倍斯特出版事業有限公司
...ning Ltd.

Learning Gram...

學文法戀習 英語寫作

文法佐茶＆情詩邂逅

說文解詩，浪漫學英文文法！

許乃文◎著

當英文文法碰上情詩！

3大篇愛的必修課：

【致愛人：那些愛的關係】、【愛的恐懼與不安】、【沒有你的日子：思念】

48首英美詩人的暖心情詩，伴學文法！

經典詩句8 精選英美詩歌，概述詩句涵義，由此導入**文法觀念**。

重點句型8 解析情詩相關的英文句型，引導讀者**寫作方向**。

寫作指引8 提供英語寫作範文參考，熟悉文章的**起承轉合**。

知識補給8 補充詩人的創作背景，拓展識聞，同步提升寫作**內容**的深度與說話的涵養。

作者序
Preface

　　本書收錄的詩以情詩為主，但由於愛情有酸甜苦辣及悲歡離合，故也收錄一些比較有悲情（pathos）成份的作品，如此才符合現實的狀況。由於篇幅限制，無法把每首選出來的詩完整地以雙語方式呈現，僅能介紹其中經典的詩句。

　　本書每個單元都有一篇英文寫作範例，這是筆者的原創作品，希望能對讀者有所幫助。至於每個單元的重點句型，都是與詩中詩句及用字有關，這並不容易，因為詩的主要構成是音律節奏及意象，不是那麼著重文法上的變法，有時甚至不太符合我們所熟悉的文法規則，讀英詩時不得不注意到這一點。

許乃文 Brian Hsu

　　詩是寫作中最精粹的一種語言，也是讓很多讀者頭痛的一種文體。詩句寫得雖精短，涵義卻是廣博深遠。尤其，文章寫得像詩一般優雅更不容易，綜觀許多西洋經典的優美詩句，若是能好好將詩句中的英文句型概念，好好應用在英語寫作上，定能讓寫作能力有大幅的躍升。

　　本書主要以收錄情詩為主，考慮到愛情五味雜陳的各種面向，所以也選錄了好幾首悲情詩。每首節選的詩節後面皆搭配講解詩句的涵義與詩人的創作背景，幫助讀者對該詩有一定程度的理解。再延伸英文句型概念，給予寫作上的指引，並提供範文讓讀者參考。

　　期許透過這本書，能給予讀者另一種提升英語寫作的方法與輔助！謝謝Brian老師的用心與耐心！

編輯部

Instructions 使用說明

Unit 1
介系詞片語
拜倫《她走在美中》
Byron "She Walks in Beauty"

詳解詩句涵義
與詩人創作背景！

Classic 經典詩句

She walks in beauty, like the night
Of cloudless climes and starry skies;
And all that's best of dark and bright
Meet in her aspect and her eyes;

英國浪漫時期主要詩人之一拜倫（Lord Byron
一首為後世所津津樂道的詩，即《她走在美中》
Beauty），其中知名的詩句有：She walks in
night／Of cloudless climes and starry sk
best of dark and bright／Meet in her asp

考翻譯：她走在美中，彷彿夜晚／無雲的蒼穹
之最精華部／交匯在她的外貌與眼眸）。詩

over。

精選經典
優美詩句。

12

Unit 1 | 介系詞片語，Byron "She Walks in Beauty

說文解詩

這首詩與其說是首情詩（love poem），還不如說是對美
（beauty）的讚美。1814 年，26 歲的拜倫在一場舞會中遇見新近喪
偶、一身黑衣的表妹霍頓夫人（Lady Wilmot Horton），不禁感受到
來自繆斯女神（Muse）的靈感而寫下這首讚美之詩。這裡的美不單只
是指女人外在的美，也涵蓋自然之美和內在之美。

詞藻釋義

☆ aspect *n.* 外觀，方位，方面，觀點
　在詩中是外觀之意，不過平常比較常用來表示方面或觀點。
　Which aspects of the job do you like ?
　你喜歡工作的哪方面？
　Consider every aspect of the problem.
　考慮問題每一個面向。

☆ clime *n.* 氣候區
　主要是在文學作品中使用，不適合一般文章。

1
Part

2
Part

3
Part

搭配詞藻釋義，
解析節選詩句
的英文字彙！

13

延伸英文句型概念，
引導寫作方向！

提供英語寫作範本！

重點句型

介系詞片語

這首詩一開頭就說 She walks in beauty。in 後面接名詞（名詞前接或不接冠詞的意義各不相同）就是介系詞片語，這種片語通常作形容詞或副詞用，詩句裡的 in beauty 就是副詞片語，用來修飾動詞 walk。

類似句型有 walk in the park、p____ the snow、sing in the rain 等，這些介系詞片語都是副詞功____，例如 He is in the park 或 a man in the p____ 片語。

寫作指引

以這首詩為參考，我們可____不使對方感到肉麻。

邂逅一位美麗的女士後____倫把女人的美比喻為有著____仿很好的範例。

範例

Your beauty shines like stars in the sky, guiding me through the dark night. I see on your face a smile that wins my heart and a blush that glows in the dark.

Your graceful gait and dignified demeanor show all the best that can be expected of a lady. I feel the presence of a peaceful mind and an innocent heart. It is the result of days spent in goodness.

Please light a way for me with your radiant beauty. I am a soul looking for redemption in beauty. You are a ____ woman that possesses both inner and outer beau____ makes you all the more attractive amo____ get to know.

Wit____

1 Part

2 Part

3 Part

附中譯，
方便對照！

中譯

你的美麗像天空中的星星一樣閃亮，指引我度過黑夜。我在你的臉上看到打動我心的笑容，及在黑暗中發光發熱的紅暈。

你那優雅的步態和高貴的舉止，在在顯示一位淑女所能表現的最好樣態。我感受到你平靜的心靈和純真的內在，這是你長期仁慈善良的結果。

請用你的耀眼之美為我指引一條路，我是一個想在美中尋求救贖的靈魂。你是一個同時擁有外在和內在之美的女人，在我所能認識的女人當中，你因而變得更具吸引力。

愛。

目次
Contents

Part 1 致愛人：那些愛的關係

Part 2 愛的恐懼與不安

Part 3 沒有你的日子：思念

Part 1

致愛人：那些愛的關係

Unit 1
介系詞片語
拜倫《她走在美中》
Byron "She Walks in Beauty"

 **Classic 經典詩句**

> She walks in beauty, like the night
> Of cloudless climes and starry skies;
> And all that's best of dark and bright
> Meet in her aspect and her eyes;

　　英國浪漫時期主要詩人之一拜倫（Lord Byron）在 1814 年寫下一首為後世所津津樂道的詩，即《她走在美中》（She Walks in Beauty），其中知名的詩句有：She walks in beauty, like the night / Of cloudless climes and starry skies; / And all that's best of dark and bright / Meet in her aspect and her eyes（參考翻譯：她走在美中，彷彿夜晚／無雲的蒼穹與滿天星星／暗黑與光明之最精華部／交匯在她的外貌與眼眸）。詩中反覆出現的 o'er 就是 over。

 說文解詩

　　這首詩與其說是首情詩（love poem），還不如說是對美（beauty）的讚美。1814 年，26 歲的拜倫在一場舞會中遇見新近喪偶、一身黑衣的表妹霍頓夫人（Lady Wilmot Horton），不禁感受到來自繆斯女神（Muse）的靈感而寫下這首讚美之詩。這裡的美不單只是指女人外在的美，也涵蓋自然之美和內在之美。

 詞藻釋義

☆ **aspect**　*n.*　外觀，方位，方面，觀點

在詩中是外觀之意，不過平常比較常用來表示方面或觀點。

Which aspects of the job do you like？

你喜歡工作的哪方面？

Consider every aspect of the problem.

考慮問題每一個面向。

☆ **clime**　*n.*　氣候區

主要是在文學作品中使用，不適合一般文章。

重點句型

介系詞片語

　　這首詩一開頭就說 She walks in beauty。in 後面接名詞（名詞前接或不接冠詞的意義各不相同）就是介系詞片語，這種片語通常作形容詞或副詞用，詩句裡的 in beauty 就是副詞片語，用來修飾動詞 walk。

　　類似句型有 walk in the park、play in the snow、sing in the rain 等，這些介系詞片語都是副詞功能，但也可作形容詞用，例如 He is in the park 或 a man in the park 中的 in the park 就是形容詞片語。

寫作指引

　　以這首詩為參考，我們可寫出一些讚美女人的英文句子，但要注意不使對方感到肉麻。

　　邂逅一位美麗的女士後，要如何用文字表達對她的仰慕和讚美？拜倫把女人的美比喻為有著無雲蒼穹和滿天星星的夜晚，就是一種可供模仿很好的範例。

範例

Your beauty shines like stars in the sky, guiding me through the dark night. I see on your face a smile that wins my heart and a blush that glows in the dark.

Your graceful gait and dignified demeanor show all the best that can be expected of a lady. I feel the presence of a peaceful mind and an innocent heart. It is the result of days spent in goodness.

Please light a way for me with your radiant beauty. I am a soul looking for redemption in beauty. You are a woman that possesses both inner and outer beauty, which makes you all the more attractive among women that I can get to know.

With love.

中譯

　　妳的美麗像天空中的星星一樣閃亮，指引我度過黑夜。我在妳的臉上看到打動我心的笑容，及在黑暗中發光發熱的紅暈。

　　妳那優雅的步態和高貴的舉止，在在顯示一位淑女所能表現的最好樣態。我感受到妳平靜的心靈和純真的內在，這是妳長期仁慈善良的結果。

　　請用妳的耀眼之美為我指引一條路，我是一個想在美中尋求救贖的靈魂。妳是一個同時擁有外在和內在之美的女人，在我所能認識的女人當中，妳因而變得更具吸引力。

　　愛。

知識補給

英國詩人喬治・戈登・拜倫（George Gordon Byron，1788-1824）人稱「拜倫勳爵」（Lord Byron），為英國 18 世紀末期至19 世紀前數十年浪漫時期的重要詩人之一，以《恰爾德・哈羅爾德遊記》和《唐璜》等長篇詩作聞名，《她走在美中》算是小品，這首詩寫於 1814 年，1815 年出版，收錄在名為《希伯來詠唱詩》的詩集中，顧名思義，詩集中的詩可以譜成曲子，這是《她走在美中》之所以成名並傳唱至今的原因之一，有興趣者可至 YouTube 搜尋以這首詩為詞的歌曲。詩的頭兩行 She walks in beauty, like the night / Of cloudless climes and starry skies 最為人所熟知，予人一種崇高（sublime）之感，但事實上，詩人營造出的崇高意象是從女子身上所穿的黑衣及黑衣上的閃亮飾片引申出來。

Unit 2

感嘆句
湯瑪士・哈代《我多麼地悲傷》
Thomas Hardy "How Great My Grief"

Classic 經典詩句

How great my grief, my joys how few,
Since first it was my fate to know thee!
- Have the slow years not brought to view
How great my grief, my joys how few

　　《我多麼地悲傷》是英國維多利亞時期小說家暨詩人湯瑪士・哈代（Thomas Hardy）所寫的一首八行兩韻詩（triolet），其中最知名的詩句為：我多麼地悲傷，歡樂多麼地少／自從命中注定認識妳／再漫長的時間也顯不出／我多麼地悲傷，歡樂多麼地少（How great my grief, my joys how few, / Since first it was my fate to know thee! / Have the slow years not brought to view / How great my grief, my joys how few）。thee 在古英文中是你或妳的意思，為受格，主格是 thou。

 說文解詩

　　這首詩是比較罕見的八行兩韻詩，短短八行中第一、第四及第七行相同，第二行及第八行相同，八行兩韻詩就是這種形式。哈代用這種反覆的形式來表達出對失去的愛的悲傷，也就是反覆用「我多麼地悲傷，歡樂多麼地少」來漸次強化及變化悲傷的情緒。

詞藻釋義

☆ grief　*n.*　悲痛，悲傷

grief 剛好和 joy 相對，人生的歡樂悲傷可用 the joys and griefs of our lives 來表達，悲痛不已則是 be overcome with grief。

☆ fate　*n.*　命運，天命

詩中用 fate 來表達命運的安排。

It was fate that brought the couple together.

命運把這一對安排在一起。

重點句型

感嘆句

這首詩中反覆出現的 How great my grief, my joys how few，是感嘆句。感嘆句的句首通常是 how 或 what，句尾再加上感嘆號。

例句：

How great you are! What a beautiful girl she is!

以 how 為首的感嘆句，詞序為 how+形容詞／副詞+主詞+動詞。

What a beautiful girl she is!

以 what 為首的感嘆句，詞序為 what+a／an+形容詞+名詞+主詞+動詞。如果用 how 來表達，就會是 How beautiful a girl she is!常見的感嘆句有 How strange!和 What a surprise!

寫作指引

愛情有機運的成分，也有命定的成分，端看出發的角度為何，愛得深，就像是命定，愛得輕鬆，就像是機運。

男方為了表達對女方的愛意，搬出了命中注定相愛之說，來讓女方更為篤定。愛的表達方式或許經常是非理性的，但為何會相愛，卻是有脈絡可循，或可歸之為命定。

範例

What is love? Is love decided by fate? Or do we fall in love by chance?

There doesn't seem to be a definite answer, depending in part on how much you love.

My love for you is a perfect example of love decided by fate. Remember the day we first met? I lost my way as looking for a friend's house. You happened to be the only passer-by that I could find. It might be a chance meeting at the beginning, but after we talked to each other for a while, I felt that something had drawn us together.

With love.

中譯

　　什麼是愛情？愛情是命運決定的嗎？或者我們是因為機緣才彼此相愛？

　　這似乎沒有絕對的答案，某部份要看你愛得有多深而定。

　　我愛上妳就是命中注定相愛的一個完美例子。還記得我們第一次相遇的那一天？我當時在找朋友住的地方，卻迷了路。妳剛好是我唯一可以找到的路人。一開始或許是偶然相遇，但彼此交談一陣子後，我感到某種東西把我們拉在一起。

　　愛。

知識補給

　　湯瑪士‧哈代（1840-1928）比較為人熟知的作品是曾改編成電影的小說《黛絲姑娘》（Tess of the d'Urbervilles），但他一直有在創作詩，只是他的詩作沒有像小說一樣那麼受到重視。《我多麼地悲傷》這首詩表達出詩人的悲傷，他的悲傷來自失去的愛人，儘管過了若干年，也無法停止悲傷。就算和其他人交往也無濟於事，詩人不斷提及的 thee，也就是他呼喚的對象，其實就是他過去的愛人，但她對詩人的呼喚和感嘆似乎無動於衷（或許不在了），這讓 How great my grief, my joys how few 的反覆出現有著逐漸強化的情緒，讀者感受到詩人越來越強的悲苦和無奈。

Unit 3

雙重否定句
雪萊《愛的哲學》
Shelley "Love's Philosophy"

Classic 經典詩句

Nothing in the world is single;

All things by a law divine

In one spirit meet and mingle.

Why not I with thine?—

　　和拜倫一樣，波西・比希・雪萊（Percy Bysshe Shelley）也是英國浪漫時期詩人，這首《愛的哲學》以萬物相互關聯的理論來敦促所愛的人接納他的愛並親吻他，著名的詩句為：世上絕無單獨存在之物；／所有事物在神聖律法下／相會並交融於單一靈魂。／為何不能與妳的靈魂交會？（Nothing in the world is single; / All things by a law divine / In one spirit meet and mingle. / Why not I with thine?—）。thine 是古早英文中你／妳的意思，是 thou 的所有格。

何謂愛？這首詩沒有給予定義，但在萬物相關聯的原則下，泉水與河流相會，河水與海洋相會，天空中的風相互交融，世界的萬物無法獨自存在，神聖的律法使大家交會融合在一個靈體之中，像是我們所說的你泥中有我，我泥中有你。

☆ single　*adj.*　單一的，單個的；個別的

現在比較常用來表示單身，例如：

He / She is single. He / She lives a single life.

single parent family 則是單親家庭。

☆ divine　*adj.*　神的，神性的

詩中的 a law divine 在正常狀況下應該以 a divine law 的方式來表達，但為了達到押韻或節奏效果，英文詩中常出現形容詞擺在名詞後面，這或許也是因為受到法文等拉丁語系語言的影響。

☆ thine　*pron.*　你的，你的東西或家屬

早年英文是用 thou 來表示 you，用 thine 來表示 your 或 yours。

重點句型

雙重否定句

詩中用到 nothing 這個字，意思是無事或無物，詞性為英文八大詞性中的代名詞，為一種雙重否定，就是沒有任何東西或事物，雙重否定就成了肯定，有時可用 not anything 來代替。

要注意的是，nothing 經常放在句首，例如，Nothing matters. 此時就不能用 not anything 來代替，如果是在句中或句尾就 OK。另外，nothing 已經是雙重否定，不能再和 not 一起出現，例如，不能說 Nothing doesn't matter.

寫作指引

愛情除了有命定之說外，另一個說法是，每一個體都無法單獨存在，且有相對應的對象。

這篇文章意圖說服習慣單身狀態女子接受新的戀情，重點在於沒人可以單獨生存這套說法，更具說服力的是沒有該名女子的親吻，生命將停止顫動。

1
Part

2
Part

3
Part

範例

"No man is an island," a famous quote from the prose by 17th century English writer John Donne, tells us that no one can be isolated from other people. It is especially true in love relationships.

You may feel comfortable about being single, but that's only for now. Cherish the moments we had together. Don't you feel that we are attracted to each other in a way that is new to you?

I have come to realize that my life won't be complete without you. And my heart won't beat without your kiss.

With Love.

中譯

　　17 世紀英國作家約翰‧鄧恩寫下「沒有人可以是個孤獨的島嶼」這個著名的句子，是在告訴我們沒人可以與其他人分隔開來，愛情關係尤其如此。

　　妳或許對單身狀態感到舒適，但那只是這個當下。珍惜我們在一起的時光。妳不覺得我們正以一種對妳來說是嶄新的方式相互吸引著？

　　我逐漸理解到，沒有妳我的生命將無法完整，沒有妳的吻我的心將不再跳動。

　　愛。

 知識補給

　　雪萊（1792-1822）和拜倫一樣是英國浪漫時期的主要詩人，兩人另一相似之處是都是英年早逝，他們都屬於一個稱為靈視派詩人（visionary poets）小團體。雪萊的妻子瑪麗就是小說《科學怪人》（Frankenstein）的作者，現在一般人比較熟悉根據這部小說改編的電影。雪萊最為人所知的詩作之一是《西風頌》（Ode to the West Wind），其中最有名的詩句是：如果冬天來了，春天還會遠嗎？（If Winter comes, can Spring be far behind?）《愛的哲學》是他的另一首好詩，裡面巧妙地運用萬物相關聯的理論來推出一個合理的結果，就是要詩人所愛之人與他交融在一起，且如果妳不親吻我，所有美好事物還有什麼價值？

Unit 4
分詞形容詞
葉慈《當妳年老時》
Yeats "When You Are Old"

Classic 經典詩句

When you are old and grey and full of sleep,

And nodding by the fire, take down this book,

And slowly read, and dream of the soft look

Your eyes had once, and of their shadows deep

...

But one man loved the pilgrim soul in you,

And loved the sorrows of your changing face

1923 年諾貝爾文學獎得主愛爾蘭詩人葉慈（W.B.Yeats）於 1891 年寫下這首傳頌至今的《當你年老時》，古人所謂寄情於詩，這首詩剛好反映出葉慈當年被心儀女性拒絕後的心情，其中著名的詩句為：When you are old and grey and full of sleep, / And nodding by the fire, take down this book, / And slowly read, and dream of the soft look / Your eyes had once, and of their

shadows deep（當年老、灰髮、昏昏欲睡的妳／在爐火旁打瞌睡時，拿起這本書／慢慢地閱讀，夢想起妳的雙眸／曾經有過的柔和模樣和深深陰鬱）。本章節則要討論以下詩句內含的文法：But one man loved the pilgrim soul in you, / And loved the sorrows of your changing face（但有個男人深愛著你那朝聖者的靈魂／愛著你那改變中的容貌之憂傷）。

　　葉慈在這首詩中化身為一個對著某位女性說話的詩人，這位女性就是愛爾蘭著名的女性革命領袖莫德‧岡（Maud Gonne），她拒絕了葉慈的追求，詩中的垂垂老矣女性就是以她為藍本。她年輕時具有迷人的風采（glad grace），但詩人就愛她內在的朝聖者靈魂（pilgrim soul）。

☆ **grey**　　*adj.*　　灰色的，頭髮灰白的
　　詩中指的是灰白的頭髮。

☆ **nod**　　*v.*　　點頭，打盹，打瞌睡
　　詩中指的是打瞌睡，nodding 是其現在分詞。

分詞形容詞

　　詩中 your changing face（妳那改變中的容貌）的 changing 是一種修飾名詞的現在分詞，稱為分詞形容詞，常見的有 the rising sun（日出）、the setting sun（日落）、breaking news（即時新聞）、boiling water（滾熱的水）等，這些是現在分詞。

　　也有過去分詞形容詞，像是 boiled egg（煮熟的蛋）、frozen food（冷凍食品）、used car（中古車）、smoked salmon（燻鮭魚）、iced tea（冰茶）等。your changing face 也可以用 your changed face 來代替，但意思是已經改變的容貌。

　　時間是女人的最大敵人，年輕時再美，年紀一到就風華不再，但我們不能只看負面的意義，也要呈現正面的能量，也就是內在美。

　　追求年輕漂亮的女性，鐵定有很多的競爭者，如何才能擊敗對手贏得美人的芳心？如果不是高富帥，就只能強調自己的內在。

範例

1
Part

2
Part

3
Part

When you are young and beautiful, you have a lot of admirers. Unlike other admirers, I like you not just for your physical beauty.

I love the pure soul in you, which will not change with age. Others might leave you when you are old, but I won't. I admire your inner beauty, which will only become more attractive with age.

It is not easy to find a true admirer like me nowadays. I may not be the most handsome or the richest among your many admirers, but I will love you till the end of my life.

With love.

中譯

當妳年輕又美麗時，妳有很多的愛慕者。和其他愛慕者不同的是，我不只是喜歡妳外表的美麗。

我愛著妳那純潔、不隨年紀變化的靈魂。當妳變老時，其他人或許會離妳而去，但我不會。我欣賞妳的內在美，那是一種越陳越香的美。

現在很難找到像我這樣的愛慕者，我或許不是妳眾多愛慕者中最帥最有錢的一個，但我會愛妳愛到生命的盡頭。

愛。

 知識補給

　　葉慈（1865-1939）是第一位獲得諾貝爾文學獎如此殊榮的愛爾蘭人，由於是以英文創作，他也是 20 世紀最重要的英國文學家之一，他的一些詩作，如《當妳年老時》、《自我與靈魂的對話》、《航向拜占庭》、《茵夢湖島》等，都是英國文學課堂上必讀的作品，由此可見他的文學地位。葉慈在《當妳年老時》中成功地營造出一個垂垂老矣的女人意象，雖然有年華老去之嘆，但仍有一個男人愛著她朝聖者般的靈魂，愛著在她變化中的容貌所看到的憂傷。他不是只愛她年輕時的美貌及迷人的風采，而是她的內在，因此在她年華老去枯坐爐火旁之際，他昇華成天上守護她的繁星之一。

Unit 5

被動句
艾佛列德・喬伊斯・基爾默《樹》
Alfred Joyce Kilmer "Trees"

Classic 經典詩句

I think I shall never see

A poem lovely as a tree

A tree whose hungry mouth is pressed

Against the earth's sweet flowing breast.

美國詩人艾佛列德・喬伊斯・基爾默（Alfred Joyce Kilmer）在
1914 年出版的詩集中收錄了這首抒情詩《樹》，其中著名的詩句為：
I think I shall never see / A poem lovely as a tree / A tree
whose hungry mouth is pressed / Against the earth's sweet
flowing breast（我想我將永遠看不到／一首和樹一樣美好的詩／這株
樹飢餓地把嘴緊貼著／大地甜美流動的胸部）。

 說文解詩

這首詩藉由讚美樹木來讚美大自然及造物主，詩人在讚美之餘不忘自我謙卑地強調，詩是他這種傻子作出來的，只有上帝才能造出樹木。樹木依靠大地的養分才能生存下來，詩人用飢餓的嘴緊貼著流著奶水的胸脯意象，來隱喻人類也同樣要靠母親的奶水才能存活下來，形容的相當生動。

 詞藻釋義

☆ **press** *v.* 按，壓，擠

做按壓動作就是用這個字，例如：

press the button to start the engine or turn on the light

☆ **breast** *n.* 乳房，胸部

詩中被用來比喻表面積雪的樹幹，可指乳房，也可指胸部。

被動句

這首詩用到了 be 動詞+過去分詞的被動式句型，像是 whose hungry mouth is pressed against。

被動式句型在強調動作接收者，例如：The girl painted the picture. 這個句子可改成被動句 The picture was painted by the girl.前者重點在動作執行者，後者重點在動作接受者，即繪畫。

被動式句型不一定要提動作施行者，例如：Breakfast is served between 7:00 and 9:00 a.m.這裡不用說 is served by who，因為重點在於早餐。

戀愛過程雖然還沒達到結婚後孕育生命的階段，但愛的本身也能產生很多正面的能量，愛的人和被愛的人都能受惠。

追求女性並不見得一定要以得到她為終極的目標，戀愛本身就能讓一個人感到愉快和幸福，輕輕鬆鬆地談一場戀愛或許也是一種不錯的選擇。

範例

1 *Part*

2 *Part*

3 *Part*

Love is the most beautiful thing in the world. It can comfort lonely souls and provide a shelter from hardship. But perfect love is rare indeed. Don't be afraid to fall in love just because it is hard to find a perfect love.

Falling in love in itself is worth the effort since one feels a sense of euphoria throughout the process.

It doesn't matter whether you marry the one you love. What matters is the process of loving someone. Why not accept my love and enjoy the feeling of being loved?

With love.

中譯

　　愛是世上最美好的事物，能安撫寂寞的心靈，暫時脫離困頓。但真愛確實稀少，別因為真愛難尋而恐懼戀愛。

　　墜入情場本身就值得所有的付出，因為可以在過程中感受到一種幸福之情。

　　是否與自己所愛的人結婚並不是最重要的事，重要的是愛的過程。何不接受我的愛享受其中的樂趣？

　　愛。

 知識補給

　　艾佛列德‧喬伊斯‧基爾默（1886-1918）是 20 世紀初期美國重要作家之一，不過由於英年早逝，所留下的作品並不多，其中最有名的就是《樹》這首詩。他喜歡讚美大自然之美，也經常流露出他的宗教信仰（他是羅馬天主教教徒）。宗教信仰過去是英國和美國文學反覆出現的重要主題，我們在探討那些時期的作品免不了要接觸到基督教信仰，而不是我們刻意所選。作為一個詩人，基爾默被評論家批評為作品過於簡單及多愁善感，或許可從《樹》這首短詩看出一些端倪，但對於我們這些外國人來說，難易度卻是剛好，不算太難，也不算太簡單。1918 年一次大戰期間，他死於法國戰場。

Unit 6
對等連接詞
柔伊・艾金斯《我是風》
Zoe Akins "I Am The Wind"

Classic 經典詩句

I am the wind that wavers,

You are the certain land;

I am the shadow that passes

Over the sand.

　　活躍於 20 世紀前半葉的美國文學家柔伊・艾金斯（Zoe Akins）在《我是風》中歌頌大自然的永恆不變，著名的詩句為：I am the wind that wavers, / You are the certain land; / I am the shadow that passes / Over the sand（我是飄動的風／你是恆定的地／我是飄過沙土／上方的陰影）。

 說文解詩

　　和永恆不變的大自然相比，人類顯得短暫易變。和恆定的大地相比，我們是飄動的風。和不動的樹木相比，我們是搖擺的樹葉。和天上固定的星星相比，我們是流動的海洋。和永恆的光芒相比，我們是會熄滅的火炬。大自然是深沈的音樂，我們只是一陣叫聲。

 詞藻釋義

☆ **waver**　*v.*　搖擺，搖晃，搖曳

通常是指樹葉或火焰在風中搖曳，也表示人的猶豫不決。

☆ **certain**　*adj.*　確定的，可靠的，一定的

詩中指的是恆定不變的大地。

重點句型

對等連接詞

　　對等連接詞 and、but 及 or 連接兩個句子時，通常可省略第二個句子重複的部分。詩中 I am the wind that wavers / You are the certain land 這兩個詩行，用散文形式來寫就要在兩個可單獨存在的句子之間加上 and，本來第二句子中的 are 可以省略，在下一詩節中，I am the leaf that quivers / You, the unshaken tree 這兩個詩行也是兩個可用 and 相連的對等子句，這次第二個句子中的 are 就被省略掉，為什麼同一種句型會產生不同的變化？這應該是詩人為了達到音韻上的變化。

寫作指引

　　用比喻的方式來表達愛情，可以含蓄地帶出想要強調的特點，也不會過於單調及一成不變。

　　把所愛之人比喻成月亮或風，自己則退居為配角，如此安排可讓女方感到榮耀和溫馨，體現出比喻這種修辭技巧的妙用。

範例

You are the moon that lights up the night. I am an exhausted traveller looking for a resting place. You light a way for me.

You are the wind that brings hope, and I am the land that waits for the wind to come. We are a perfect match. You can help me become a better man, and I can make you a happy woman. Isn't it wonderful?

I am making my way toward the destination. You don't need to move at all since you are the destination for me. Our love for each other decides the remaining distance.

With love.

中譯

　　妳是照亮夜晚的月亮，我則是一個找尋歇腳處的疲憊旅人。妳為我照亮了一條路。

　　妳是帶來希望的風，我則是等待風的來臨的陸地。我們是天造地設的一對。妳能讓我變得更好，我可以讓妳快樂。這不是很棒嗎？

　　我正在往目的地邁進，妳不用做任何動作，因為妳就是我的目的地。我們彼此的相愛程度決定了剩下的距離。

　　愛。

 知識補給

　　柔伊‧艾金斯（1886-1958）不但是個詩人，還編寫劇本，1935 年獲得普立茲戲劇類獎。她也為電影編寫劇本，比較知名的有 1936 年的《茶花女》（Camille），女主角就是著名影星葛麗泰‧嘉寶（Greta Garbo）。艾金斯的《我是風》是她比較為人稱道的作品，其主題除了在讚美大自然外，也凸顯出人類的渺小和無常，這種想法在我們東方人看來頗有心有戚戚焉之感，但在不斷強調征服自然的當時，或許不能算是主流思想，要來到現在這個過度使用天然資源的年代才會更覺得有道理。或許這首詩能讓人類更為謙卑，更能尊敬大自然。人定勝天一說在不同時代也有不同的解釋。

Unit 7

插入語
艾德溫・阿諾德《命定》
Edwin Arnold "Destiny"

Classic 經典詩句

Somewhere there waiteth in this world of ours

For one lone soul another lonely soul

Each choosing each through all the weary hours

And meeting strangely at one sudden goal.

Then blend they, like green leaves with golden flowers,

Into one beautiful and perfect whole.

19 世紀英國詩人艾德溫・阿諾德（Edwin Arnold）的詩作《命定》讓人有東方思維之感，原來阿諾德曾經在英國統治印度時期在印度待了 6 年。這首 8 行詩的著名詩句為：Somewhere there waiteth in this world of ours / For one lone soul another lonely soul / Each choosing each through all the weary hours / And meeting strangely at one sudden goal / Then blend they, like green leaves with golden flowers, / Into one beautiful and

perfect whole.（在我們這個世界的某處／一個孤獨的靈魂等著另一個／經過這麼久的乏味時間才相互選擇到／並奇妙地在某個突然的目標物上相遇／像是綠葉陪襯金色的花蕊／結合為一個漂亮完美的整體）。

說文解詩

　　每個孤獨的人都會在世界某個地方等待另一個孤獨的人，但之前都要先經歷一段枯燥乏味的時光，才會相互選擇到彼此，並在某個突然出現的目標物上相遇。接著他們就像綠葉和金花一樣結合在一起，成為一個美麗完美的整體，此時生命的漫漫長夜已然結束，展開在眼前的是通往永恆白晝之路。

詞藻釋義

☆ lone　*adj.*　孤單的，無伴的
　　詩中的 lone soul 和 lonely soul 都是孤獨的靈魂之意（或人，以前英文常用 soul 來表示人）。

☆ weary　*adj.*　疲倦的，疲勞的
　　和 tired 有類似的意義，但 tired 是體力或精力耗損後產生的疲倦，weary 則是無由來的疲倦。

 **重點句型**

插入語

　　英文句子中經常插入一些不影響句子獨立性的補充說明詞語、片語或子句，這些插入語前後要用逗號與所補充說明的句子分開，它們不影響句子的文法完整性，去掉也可以。

　　詩句 Then blend they, like green leaves with golden flowers, / Into one beautiful and perfect whole 中的 like green leaves with gold flowers 就是這類的插入語，目的是豐富原來的句義。類似的例子還有：His father, fortunately, was rescued from the burning car wreck.或 Regular exercise, I think, is good for your health.

寫作指引

　　命中注定相愛有不同的表達方式，可以是一開始就註定了某一特定的對象，也可以是遲早一定會碰到對象，但這個對象並沒有預先注定好。

　　讓自己所追求的女子了解到她是你在等待的對象，一些修辭問句不是要她做任何回答，而是更為凸顯你所想要的答案。

範例

Somewhere in the world, there is always someone waiting for you. I didn't know who that someone was until I met you.

Was it some kind of destiny? Do you believe in this kind of theory? I do. More precisely, I felt I was very lucky to meet you. It will be better if you feel likewise.

I wish to extend my luck days indefinitely. Whether my wish could come true is up to you. My future is in your hands. It is indeed my destiny to know you.

With love.

中譯

　　在世界某個地方總有個人在等你。我不曉得那個人是誰，直到遇見了妳。

　　那是一種命定嗎？妳相信這種理論嗎？我相信。更確切的是，我覺得自己很幸運才到遇見妳。妳如果也是這麼想，就更好。

　　我希望無限期延長我的幸運日，我的願望是否能實現取決於妳。我的未來掌握在妳的手上，我真的是命中注定才會遇見妳。

　　愛。

 知識補給

　　艾德溫‧阿諾德（1832-1904）除了詩人身份外，還擔任過記者，最有名的作品是長篇敘事詩《亞洲之光》（The Light of Asia），主題是悉達哈王子悟道成為佛祖的歷程。阿諾德在印度待過 6 年，從他的作品可看出東方思想對他的影響。《命定》這首詩提到孤獨的靈魂會在某處等到另一個孤獨的靈魂，這似乎就是所謂的命定，或是中國思想中常提到命中注定的觀念。阿諾德另一讓後人稱道之事，是在擔任英國每日電訊報（Daily Telegraph）編輯期間，曾安排著名探險家史丹利（H.M. Stanley）赴非洲探險，進而發現了剛果河流域，這在當時可是一件大事。史丹利的探險故事啟發了小說家康拉德（Joseph Conrad），使他寫下小說《黑暗之心》（Heart of Darkness）。

Unit 8
感官動詞
威廉・沃茲沃斯《孤獨的割禾女》
William Wordsworth "The Solitary Reaper"

Classic 經典詩句

Behold her, single in the field,

Yon solitary Highland Lass!

Reaping and singing by herself;

Stop here, or gently pass!

...

I saw her singing at her work,

And o'er the sickle bending

　　19 世紀英國浪漫派大詩人威廉・沃茲沃斯（William Wordsworth）這首《孤獨的割禾女》中既歌頌自然之美，也讚嘆人聲之美，其中著名的詩句為：Behold her, single in the field, / Yon solitary Highland Lass! / Reaping and singing by herself; / Stop here, or gently pass!（瞧孤立在田裡的她／那邊孤獨的高地少

女／獨自邊收割邊唱歌／要嘛駐足聆聽，要嘛輕輕走過！）。本章節則要討論以下詩句內含的文法：I saw her singing at her work, / And o'er the sickle bending（我看見她邊唱邊幹活／彎著腰，揮動鐮刀）。

 說文解詩

　　這首詩描述詩人在蘇格蘭高地旅行時，遇見獨自在田裡收割農作物的少女，他為她所唱的悲傷曲調所吸引，諾大的谷地瀰漫著她的歌聲。她的歌聲比夜鶯的啼叫更能讓疲憊的旅者感到舒暢，詩人從頭到尾都不知道她在唱什麼，即使在逐漸走遠之後，仍感到她的歌聲在自己的心裡迴響。

 詞藻釋義

☆ behold　*v.* 看，看見　*int.* 瞧，看呀
　　這是比較文雅及古早的用詞，相當於現代英文的 look。

☆ solitary　*adj.* 單獨的，獨自的，孤獨的，寂寞的
　　詩中應該是獨自的之意，因為唱歌的女孩看不出有孤獨或寂寞的樣子。

感官動詞

I saw her singing at her work. 這個句子運用到感官動詞＋受詞＋現在分詞句型，感官動詞有 see、look at、hear、listen to、feel 等，後面可接原形動詞或現在分詞。

原形動詞是表示看到或聽到某一動作的發生，現在分詞是強調該動作的發生過程。

如果用 I saw her sing at her work. 來代替原來的句子，就表現不出現在正在發生的動作。感官動詞後面也可以接過去分詞，表示受詞所接收的動作。

情書除了表達愛意外，也可以讚美對方的才華，像是唱歌和舞蹈方面的才藝。

讚美是一種美德，更能在戀愛時發揮功效。古人把女人的歌聲比喻為黃鶯出谷，我們現代人要想些新的詞語來表達。

範例

1
Part

2
Part

3
Part

I remember I was first attracted by the sound of your voice, which is pleasing to the ear and soothing to the soul.

You were singing in a singing contest. I was amazed at the beauty of your voice. You were singing a French song. I didn't know what the song was about. It might be a love song. Whatever the theme was, the song greatly appealed to my emotions.

You might not remember that there was a guy in the audience staring at you with his mouth wide open. Or there might be more than one guy with the same expression on his face.

With love.

中譯

　　我記得一開始是被妳的聲音所吸引，那是一種悅耳、撫慰心靈的聲音。

　　妳當時在參加歌唱比賽，妳的歌聲讓我驚為天人。妳唱的是一首法文歌，我不知道歌曲的內容，也許是首情歌，但它大大地牽動了我的情緒。

　　妳或許不記得觀眾席中有人張著大嘴盯著妳看，或許當時有同樣表情的人不只一人。

　　愛。

知識補給

　　英國浪漫派大詩人威廉・沃茲沃斯（1770-1850）和同時期詩人柯勒律芝（Samuel Taylor Coleridge）共同發起英國文學史上的浪漫主義運動，他們共同創作的《抒情歌謠集》（Lyrical Ballads）於1798 年出版，成為英國文學浪漫時期的濫觴。沃茲沃斯和拜倫、雪萊及濟慈等其他浪漫派詩人不同的是，他活得很久，且創作量極大。《孤獨的割禾女》算是沃茲沃斯比較知名的作品之一，1805 年創作，1807 年出版。有趣的是，這首詩不是沃茲沃斯的個人經驗，而是根據湯瑪士・威金森（Thomas Wilkinson）所寫的《不列顛山脈遊記》（Tours to the British Mountains），這有點出乎我們的意料之外。沃茲沃斯從 1843 年起擔任英國的桂冠詩人（Poet Laureate），直到 1850 年去世為止。

1
Part

2
Part

3
Part

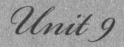

Unit 9
關係代名詞 they who / people who
瓦爾特・拉雷爵士《沈默的愛人》
Sir Walter Raleigh "The Silent Lover"

Classic 經典詩句

Passions are liken'd best to floods and streams:
The shallow murmur, but the deep are dumb

...

They that are rich in words, in words discover
That they are poor in that which makes a lover.

瓦爾特・拉雷爵士（Sir Walter Raleigh）是英國伊莉莎白時代著名的探險家，也是位作家、詩人、軍人、政治家，他的詩作不算多，《沈默的愛人》是他比較著名的一首，其中著名的詩句為：Passions are liken'd best to floods and streams: / The shallow murmur, but the deep are dumb（把激情比喻為洪水和溪流最佳／淺水潺潺作響，但深水寂靜無聲）。本章節則要討論以下詩句內含的文法：They that are rich in words, in words discover / That they are poor in that which makes a lover.（善於甜言蜜語的，實則虛情假意。）

 說文解詩

　　詩人把激情比喻為洪水和溪流，算是少見，但看了之後才覺得比喻得真好。淺水發出的聲音大，深水卻沒有聲音，意思是用情不深的人聲音最大；詞藻豐富的人會在他們的詞藻裡發現，他們缺乏愛人之所為愛人的特質。

詞藻釋義

☆ **liken** *v.* 把……比作
be likened to 是被比喻為
She's likened to a young Marilyn Monroe.
她被比作年輕的瑪麗蓮夢露。

☆ **shallow** *adj.* 淺的，淺薄的，膚淺的
詩中同時指淺的和膚淺的。

☆ **murmur** *n.* 輕柔持續的聲音，沙沙聲，潺潺聲，低語聲
詩中同時指持續的潺潺水聲和人的低語聲。

 重點句型

關係代名詞 *they who / people who*

詩中的 they that are rich in words 用到 they who 這個句型，they that 是比較老的用法，但在聖經的英文譯文及詩歌中仍有用到，所以還是要認識一下。

現在通常用 they who 和 people who，也可用單數的 he who 或 anyone who 來表達相同的意思。

例如：
God helps those who help themselves.
句子裡的 who 可以用 that 來代替，those who have money、people who have money、he who has money、anyone who has money 或 she who has money 的意思都一樣，只有單複數的差別。

 寫作指引

愛情的傳遞不在於文藻的華麗，而在於真情的表達，除了一些基本的修辭技巧外，勿過度賣弄文字技巧。

追求女性當然要用文字來表達，但過度依賴文字會讓女方深陷於文字所帶來的假象，表達真實的情感才是正事。

範例

What is true love? Do you fall in love with sweet words or with the person who says those words? Or both?

Those who are rich in words might be poor in what makes true love. Don't fall in love with language. Take a good look at the admirers surrounding you, and you'll find who really loves you.

If you have time, read through the letters I have sent to you. They might not be beautifully worded, but do convey my true feelings. I greatly admire your candidness and sincerity because I have the same character.

With love.

中譯

何謂真愛？妳愛上的是甜言蜜語還是說出這些話語的人？或是都有？

富於詞藻的人或許缺乏構成真愛的特質，不要愛上言語。好好看看妳身邊的愛慕者，就可以發現誰真的愛妳。

妳如果有空，可以讀讀我捐給妳的信，我寫的信雖然文藻並不華麗，卻傳達出真實的感情。我極為欣賞妳的率真和真誠，因為我的個性也是如此。

愛。

知識補給

　　瓦爾特‧拉雷爵士（1552-1618）是個傳奇性人物，不只能創作文學作品和寫書，還帶領探險隊到美洲探險，1584 年在北美洲成立維吉尼亞殖民地，以歌頌當時的英國女王伊莉莎白一世。伊莉莎白女王對他的寵愛更是為人所津津樂道，近年以伊莉莎白一世為主題的電影都有彰顯他們兩人之間的關係。一生多采多姿的拉雷爵士，在文學上的地位不是很顯著，某些詩作甚至被人拿來當成劣詩的範本，但就這首《沈默的愛人》而言，他還是頗有詩才，不能僅以他的一些失敗作品來否定他的所有作品。儘管有著豐功偉業，拉雷爵士卻三次入獄，第一次是因為得罪了伊莉莎白女王，第二次和第三次都是在繼任的詹姆士一世國王任內，第三次入獄時終難逃一死。

Unit 10
假設語氣
克里斯多福・馬羅《熱情牧人情歌》
Christopher Marlowe "The Passionate Shepherd to His Love"

Classic 經典詩句

Come live with me and be my love,
And we will all the pleasures prove
That valleys, groves, hills, and fields,
Woods, or steepy mountain yields.

...

And if these pleasures may thee move,
Come live with me and be my love.

16 世紀英國伊莉莎白時期文學家克里斯多福・馬羅（Christopher Marlowe）的這首《熱情牧人情歌》於 1599 年出版，也就是在馬羅死後才出版。它是一首田園詩（pastoral），其中著名的詩句為：Come live with me and be my love, / And we will all the pleasures prove / That valleys, groves, hills, and fields, / Woods, or steepy mountain yields.（來和我一起住當我

的愛人／我們將探索所有好玩的地方／不論是山谷、樹叢、丘陵、田野／還是樹林或陡峭的群山）。本章節則要討論以下詩句內含的文法：And if these pleasure may thee move, / Come live with me and be my love.（如果這一切能討妳歡心／來和我一起住當我的愛人。）

 說文解詩

　　詩中的牧人不斷向女方提出各種邀約，希望她能接受並成為他的愛人，所以不斷重複 Come live with me and be my love 這個句子。這些邀約包括找她到處看看、坐在河岸邊聽瀑布聲和鳥叫聲的合奏、用玫瑰為她做一張床、用樹葉為她做一件裙子，諸此等等都是為了贏得她的歡心。

 詞藻釋義

☆ grove　*n.*　樹叢，小樹林
　　詩中列舉了一連串田園名詞，如谷地、小樹林、丘陵、田野等。

☆ steepy　*adj.*　陡峭的
　　早期英文中的陡峭之意，相當於現在 steep。

重點句型

假設語氣

詩中的 if these pleasures may thee move 用到 if 句型，這個句子按照一般寫法應該是 if these pleasures may move thee，但詩人為了押韻或節奏可調整句中各個組成的位置，像是常見的倒裝句。

if 句型分成可能發生的狀況及與事實相反的狀況兩種。
例如：
If it rains tomorrow, we will cancel the trip.
這是有可能發生的狀況，所以用直述句方式呈現。
If I had a lot of money, I would buy a luxury car.
這是與現在事實相反的狀況，所以用假設語氣。

寫作指引

為愛人營造出一幅田園的景象，許她一個願景，許她一個未來，這將給她無限的想像空間。

戀愛過程提出一個未來的規劃很重要，尤其是關於家的規劃，每個女人都想要一個屬於自己的家，如何規劃將會成為雙方的共同話題。

範例

What's your plan for the future? I have an idea. How about building our own house in the countryside?

The house doesn't need to be big. It will have everything we need, ranging from a cozy living room, a spacious and bright master room, a kitchen with an island, to a front yard with a landscaped garden. If you have your own idea, just put it on the list. You name it and we have it.

Of course, there is a budget limit. We'll try to get the best within the budget limit. We don't need luxury items. We'll be fine with a modest lifestyle.

With love.

中譯

　　妳對未來有何打算？我有個主意。我們到鄉間蓋一棟屬於自己的房子如何？

　　房子不用太大，只要該有的都有就好，像是舒適的客廳、寬敞明亮的主臥室、有著中島的廚房，及有庭園造景的前院。如果妳想到什麼，就加到清單上。妳說得出來，我們就會去弄到。

　　當然還是有預算限制，我們將在預算範圍內弄到最好的東西。我們不需要奢侈品，只要過著樸實的生活就好。

　　愛。

知識補給

　　克里斯多福・馬羅（1564-1593）和莎士比亞同年出生，卻比莎士比亞在戲劇創作上更早成名，由於 29 歲就死於非命，所留下的劇作並不多，但對莎士比亞產生了很大的影響，例如：馬羅的《馬爾他猶太人》（The Jew of Malta）就啟發了莎翁的《威尼斯商人》（Merchant of Venice）。馬羅在戲劇上的成就及名聲遠大於他在詩詞創作上的表現，但單就這首《熱情牧人情歌》來看，馬羅還是有相當的造詣。所謂田園詩就是把場景設定在鄉間，但所營造的是一種理想化的鄉村場景，和現實生活有段出入，而時間點也是設定在舒服的五月天，而不是令人難熬的冬天。當然這種理想化的鄉村景象無非是為了讓人聯想起人類失去的伊甸園。

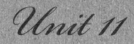

Unit 11
所有格代名詞
華特・史考特爵士《最後吟遊詩人之歌》第 5 章第 13 節
Sir Walter Scott "The Lay of the Last Minstrel. Canto V. Stanza 13"

 **Classic 經典詩句**

True love 's the gift which God has given
To man alone beneath the heaven:
It is not fantasy's hot fire,
Whose wishes soon as granted fly;

　　18 世紀後期蘇格蘭著名小説家暨詩人華特・史考特爵士（Sir Walter Scott）於 1805 年出版了長篇詩《最後吟遊詩人之歌》，其中一段談到何謂真愛，著名的詩句為：True love's the gift which God has given / To man alone beneath the heaven: / It is not fantasy's hot fire, / Whose wishes soon as granted fly（真愛是上帝賜予的禮物／賜給蒼穹之下的人類／它不是幻想的熱火／不會在願望得准之後就消散）。

 說文解詩

　　真愛是上帝賜予人類的禮物，不是幻想中的熱火，不會在願望恩准後就消逝。真愛不是存在於強烈的慾望之中，不會隨著慾望的消失而死去。它是發自內心的同情，是一種銀色的連結，一種如絲般的繩索，使雙方心心相連，肉體與心靈相結合。

 詞藻釋義

☆ fantasy　*n.*　空想，幻想，夢想

比較早期的英文是以 fantasy 來表達類似於現在 imagination 的意義，也就是幻想或想像。

☆ grant　*v.*　同意，准予，給予

詩中是給予的意思，現代英文比較常用來表達同意或准予，像是 grant a request。

重點句型

所有格代名詞

　　whose 為關係代名詞的所有格，通常是用在先行詞為人的狀況下：He has a friend whose wife is a teacher. I want to buy a book whose subject is music.第一個句子的先行詞為 a friend，第二個句子的先行詞為 a book，兩者後面的關係代名詞都要用所有格的 whose，而不是主格的 who。

　　關係代名詞可以把本來要用兩個句子才能表達出來的句子結合在一個句子內，例如：He has a friend. 和 His friend's wife is a teacher.這兩個句子可以結合成一個句子——He has a friend whose wife is a teacher.

寫作指引

　　真愛不等於肉體上的慾望，如何做一區別，男女雙方都要進行溝通，以免將兩者搞混在一起。

　　戀愛過程一定會牽涉到性愛，如果一方有所堅持，就無法產生性行為。通常是女方為了宗教信仰或家族傳統排斥婚前性行為，男方在尊重之餘也要諒解。

範例

True love is not made out of sexual desire. I do have sexual desire for you since you are physically attractive. I am just an ordinary man with natural instincts. But I agree with your view that premarital sex is not something to be encouraged.

I know how to control my desire despite still having some doubts about the necessity of such restraint. How can a man like me refrain from sexual impulses toward a woman as beautiful as you? As you have said to me, love is patient, which I found to be quoted from the Bible. It makes sense to me.

With love.

中譯

真愛不是由性慾構成。我對妳的確有性的慾望，因為妳的外表是如此地誘人。我只是一個有著本能反應的平凡男人，卻也同意妳的看法，即不該鼓勵婚前性行為。

我知道如何控制自己的慾望，儘管仍對節制慾望一事有所疑惑。我這樣一個男人如何能對妳這麼漂亮的女人克制性衝動？誠如妳對我說過的，愛是恆久忍耐，我發現這句話是出自聖經。我覺得有道理。

愛。

 知識補給

　　蘇格蘭文學家華特‧史考特爵士（1771-1832）比較為人所知的是他所創作的小說，如取材於蘇格蘭的歷史小說《威佛利》（Waverley）和以 12 世紀英格蘭為背景的《撒克遜英雄傳》（Ivanhoe）。1805 年出版的長篇詩《最後吟遊詩人之歌》是史考特在詩歌創作上的第一部成功作品，我們選錄的是其中第 5 章第 13 詩節，內容是在描述何謂真愛，真愛能使人心心相連，身體與靈魂合一。歐洲自中古時期起一直有肉體與靈魂之間的辯論，也就是把道德上的衝突或抉擇歸咎於肉體與靈魂之間的對抗，但到了史考特的時代，這種辯證或許已不存在，只要用真愛就能予以克服，而這種真愛是上帝所恩賜的（史考特的觀點）。

Unit 12
連接詞
艾蜜莉・狄更生《我總是愛著》
Emily Dickinson "That I Did Always Love"

Classic 經典詩句

That I did always love

I bring thee Proof

That till I loved

I never lived— Enough—

19 世紀美國女詩人艾蜜莉・狄更生（Emily Dickinson）在《我總是愛著》這詩中讚美愛就是生命，就是永恆。著名的詩句為：That I did always love / I bring thee Proof / That till I loved / I never lived—Enough—（我總是愛著／我帶給你證據／在我還沒愛之前／我不算活著—不夠—）。

狄更生在這首詩中讚美愛，認為愛就是生命，直到真正去愛，才算是活著，才算活得夠。要一直愛，因為愛是生命，而生命具有永恆性（immortality）。她在詩中對著說話對象說，如果你有所懷疑，我只能表現出悲哀，原文用耶穌受難像（calvary）來隱喻悲哀。

☆ proof　*n.*　證據，物證

英文常說的：The proof of the pudding is in the eating.

就是布丁好不好吃，要吃了才知道。

重點句型

連接詞

　　that 除了當關係代名詞外，還可作為連接詞。詩中的 proof that，that 是連接詞，引導出一個名詞子句，不是用來形容前面的名詞，而是作為前面名詞的同位語。例句：Do you have any proof that he stole the goods?（你有任何證據證明東西是他偷的嗎？）The news that the U.S. dollar is to depreciate against the euro is a great shock to some investors.（美元兌歐元貶值的消息對一些投資客而言是個大衝擊。）這兩個句子中的 that 都是引導名詞子句的連接詞，此時 that 不可省略也不能用其他字詞替代，某些名詞後面經常接這類 that 子句，例如：fact, truth, evidence, proof, statement, explanation, suggestion, advice, promise, opinion, notion, theory, view, conclusion, decision, news, report, rumor, saying, idea, thought, belief, doubt, knowledge 等。

寫作指引

　　詩人認為愛就是生命，就是永恆，直到真正去愛，才算是活著，這是無庸置疑的。

　　要讓女方知道你對她的愛慕，必須證明給她看，也就是要讓她看到你的心，了解你的心意，讓她知道你的心是金子做的。

範例

It is good to fall in love. It is even better to love someone for the whole of your life. Love is life. If you love someone, you love life as well.

That someone is the woman who occupies your heart. You make me feel the same way. Don't doubt my words. I'll show the proof, which lies in my heart.

Come and touch my heart. You'll find the truth. The truth is that I love you from the bottom of my heart. And my heart is a heart of gold. It is why I deserve your love.

With love.

中譯

愛是好事，用畢生的時間去愛一個人會更好。愛是生命。如果你愛上某人，你同樣也會愛上生命。

那個人是佔據你心的女人，而你就是讓我有這種感覺的女人。不要懷疑我的話，我會證明給妳看，就在我的心中。

過來碰觸我的心，妳會發現到真相，真相就是我打從心底愛上妳。我有著金子般的心，這是我值得妳的愛的原因。

愛。

知識補給

艾蜜莉‧狄更生（1830-1886）出生於麻薩諸塞州安默斯特的顯赫家族，詩作風格經常不按照傳統的格律和語法，不時提出創新的比喻和意象，算是現代派詩人的先驅，不過她生前只發表過 10 首詩，其他大量的詩作要到死後近 70 年才重新得到文學界的重視，這和她過著隱士般生活有關，她也不是為了出版作品而創作，而是為了創作而創作。她在 1860 至 1865 年間隱居起來努力創作，她雖然在詩作中讚美愛情，但她個人的感情生活卻不太為外人所知，她終身未婚，據說她喜歡年紀比較大的有學問男士，但和男人都維持一種柏拉圖式關係，有點像是在尋找異性知己或心靈上的伴侶。

Unit 13

不定詞片語
華特・惠特曼《來自翻滾的海洋，人群》
Walt Whitman "Out of the Rolling Ocean, the Crowd"

 **Classic 經典詩句**

Out of the rolling ocean, the crowd, came a drop gently to me,

Whispering, I love you, before long I die,

I have travel'd a long way, merely to look on you, to touch you

　　19 世紀美國文學家華特・惠特曼（Walt Whitman）在 1865 年寫下這首《來自翻滾的海洋，人群》，和傳統詩不同的是，這首詩沒有押韻，呈現出一種自由的表達方式。著名的詩句為：Out of the rolling ocean, the crowd, came a drop gently to me, / Whispering, I love you, before long I die, / I have travel'd a long way, merely to look on you, to touch you（來自翻滾的海洋，人群，一滴水輕輕落在我身上／低喃著，我愛你，不久我將消逝／我旅行了一大段路，只為了見到你，碰觸到你）。

 說文解詩

　　這首詩要表達的是，我們大家都是一體，都是海洋的一部份，都會找到我們鍾愛的人或事物。我們終會在海洋中相遇，但會先碰到一些阻隔或距離，儘管如此，我們不會永遠分隔，不要缺乏耐心（Be not impatient），我要向空氣、海洋及土地致敬，就在每一天的日落時分。

 詞藻釋義

☆ roll　*v.*　滾動，打滾

　一般指物體的滾動或船隻的搖晃。

☆ merely　*adv.*　只是，僅僅，不過

　意思類似 only。

　merely to touch you 是只為了碰到你的意思。

重點句型

不定詞片語

詩中的 to look on you 和 to touch you 都是不定詞片語，所謂不定詞片語就是 to+原形動詞的片語，原形動詞後面可加受詞也可不加。不定詞片語可作為名詞、形容詞或副詞之用，詩中兩個例子都是作為副詞用的不定詞片語。

例句：

She wants to go to America to study music. I am sorry to disappoint you. She is too young to marry.

作為副詞的不定詞片語通常表達為了某種目的或可以達成的事項，某些不定詞片語已成為慣用語，在句子裡作為副詞用，像是 to be sure 或 to tell you the truth。

寫作指引

談情說愛不能只談感情，也要與周遭的世界結合在一起，營造出一種整體的大愛感覺。

男女雙方都是世界的一部份，卻也同時各有各的世界，原先毫無交集，只因為有愛，雙方的世界開始產生交集。

範例

1
Part

2
Part

3
Part

We are part of the world. I have my own small world, and you have yours. The thing is, I want to be part of your world. May I?

Every night as I gaze at the stars, I feel the presence of your world. The thought of you makes me feel like in a paradise.

If I could have the access to your world, it would be like in state of bliss.

If you let me be part of your world, I'll give my whole world to you. My whole world might be a small one, but it has everything you can think of.

With love.

中譯

　　我們都是這個世界的一部份，我有我的小世界，妳也有妳的。重點是，我想要成為妳的世界的一部份，可以嗎？

　　每晚當我看著天空中的星星時，我總是感覺到妳的世界的存在，想到妳就讓我有置身天堂的感覺。

　　如果我能進入妳的世界，那會像是進入一種幸福無比的境地。

　　如果妳讓我成為妳的世界的一部份，我會把我的世界全部給妳，雖然那只是一個小小的世界，但只要妳能想到的東西都有。

　　愛。

 知識補給

　　華特‧惠特曼（1819-1892）和艾蜜莉‧狄更生現在被公認為美國 19 世紀最偉大的詩人，他最有名的作品是《草葉集》詩集，自由的創作手法讓他成為自由詩（free verse）的創始人之一，由《來自翻滾的海洋，人群》這首詩便可看出一二。除了詩人身份外，惠特曼還是個散文家及新聞工作者。在他有生之年發生了幾件改變美國歷史的事件，從美國的內戰，林肯總統被暗殺，再到加州的淘金熱。也難怪他在創作文學作品之外也關心時事投入新聞工作，他曾創辦一份報紙，並在紐約當過記者。他的詩作影響到後來的現代派詩人，像是艾茲拉‧龐德（Ezra Pound）、艾略特（T.S. Eliot）及奧登（W.H. Auden）等。

Unit 14

動詞片語
山繆爾‧泰勒‧柯勒律芝《愛情盲目的理由》
Samuel Taylor Coleridge "Reason For Love's Blindness"

 Classic 經典詩句

I have heard of reasons manifold

Why Love must needs be blind,

But this the best of all I hold--

His eyes are in his mind.

英國浪漫派大詩人山繆爾‧泰勒‧柯勒律芝（Samuel Taylor Coleridge）在《愛情盲目的理由》這首詩中解釋愛情為何是盲目的，因為是用心來看。著名的詩句為：I have heard of reasons manifold / Why Love must needs be blind, / But this the best of all I hold-- / His eyes are in his mind.（我聽過各式各樣的理由／解釋為何愛情一定是盲目的／然這是我所聽過最棒的——他的眼睛在他的心裡）。

 說文解詩

　　人們總喜歡說愛情是盲目的，這個說法從莎士比亞時代起就開始存在，莎翁在劇作《威尼斯商人》中寫道：「愛情是盲目的，情人看不到他們自己犯下的美麗愚行」。柯勒律芝在他的詩中給了答案，因為是用心來看待愛人，所以只能看到優點，無視於其他一切。

 詞藻釋義

☆ manifold　*adj.*　眾多的，五花八門的

The implications of the policy was manifold.

這個政策所蘊含的意義是多樣的。

☆ needs　*adv.*　必要地，必須地

通常是在文學作品品中出現，且要和 must 一起用。例如：

He must needs go.

他一定要走。

It must needs be so.

一定是那樣。

重點句型

動詞片語

　　詩中用到 hear of 這類不可分離雙字動詞片語，類似的動詞片語還有 dream of、think of、look at、prepare for、laugh at、look for、listen to、talk about、get into 等，這類片語後面接受詞或動名詞。

　　還有可分離的雙字動詞片語，如 find out、pick up 和 take off。

　　例如：

I pick up the book.

I pick the book up.

I pick it up.

這三種用法都可以。但不可分離的雙字動詞片語只有一種用法，I hear of the news.不能說成 I hear the news of.

寫作指引

　　大家都同意愛情是盲目的這句話，不過是全然地盲目還是選擇性地盲目，卻存在著很大的差別。

　　愛情是盲目的，也是不講道理的，所以要用誇獎對方的方式來達到說理的目的，對方在接受讚美之餘應該會接受你所說的道理。

範例

1
Part

2
Part

3
Part

People like to say, "Love is blind." It means that most people take it as a universal truth without ever giving it a second thought. What it means is rather that people tend not to see bad things about their loved ones.

I see with my heart and not with my eyes. I don't care that much about your appearance since I see with my heart. I can see that you are kind and nice. I know you treat your friends like family members.

It's what I like about you. Stay true to yourself.

With love.

中譯

　　人們喜歡說，「愛情是盲目的」，意思是大多數人不假思索就把這句話當成不變的真理，其實真正的意義是，人們傾向於看不到愛人的不好事情。

　　我是用心而不是用眼在看，我不那麼在乎妳的外表，因為我是用心在看。我看得出妳是個仁慈善良的女人，也知道妳把朋友當成家人一樣對待。

　　我衝著這一點喜歡上妳。保持忠於妳自己。

　　愛。

知識補給

　　山繆爾・泰勒・柯勒律芝（1772-1834）和威廉・沃茲沃斯同樣都是英國浪漫派大將，兩人共同發起英國文學史上的浪漫主義運動，1798 年他們所出版的共同創作《抒情歌謠集》（Lyrical Ballads），成了英國浪漫時期文學的濫觴。然柯勒律芝的詩風不同於沃茲沃斯，以《古舟子之歌》（The Rime of the Ancient Mariner）為例，柯勒律芝已從浪漫主義所崇尚的想像力（imagination）轉換到幻想（fancy），這或許和他沈溺於鴉片有關，他發揮出帶有一種超現實色彩的想像力，某種程度上已具有現代的風格。柯勒律芝還寫了一首與東方蒙古帝國有關的詩《忽必烈汗》，據說這首詩的靈感是來自他吸完鴉片後所產生的奇幻夢境。

1
Part

2
Part

3
Part

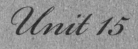

Unit 15
複合形容詞
羅伯特‧布朗寧《相遇在夜晚》
Robert Browning "Meeting at Night"

 **Classic** 經典詩句

Then a mile of warm sea-scented beach;
Three fields to cross till a farm appears;
A tap at the pane, the quick sharp scratch
And blue spurt of a lighted match,
And a voice less loud, thro' its joys and fears,
Than the two hearts beating each to each!

　　英國維多利亞時期詩人羅伯特‧布朗寧（Robert Browning）在這首詩中用生動的意象描繪出敘述者在夜晚月光的照耀下划船到愛人住處的過程，除了用到視覺的意象外，也營造出聲音的意象。例如：一個聽得出既愉悅又害怕的微小聲音／比兩個彼此相悅之人的心跳聲還小（And a voice less loud, thro' its joys and fears, / Than the two hearts beating each to each!）本章節則要討論以下詩句內含的文法：Then a mile of warm sea-scented beach; / Three

fields to cross till a farm appears（走過一哩飄海香的溫暖沙灘／越過三塊農田見一座農舍／輕扣窗櫺，尖銳地刮擦聲響／火柴迸出藍色的火光）。

 說文解詩

　　詩的一開始先描寫灰色的海和暗黑的長條陸地，顯然視覺觀點是從海上往陸地看，讀者因此得知敘述者是在海上划船。他划到一個泥濘的海灘靠岸，上岸後走了一英哩並穿越三處牧場後來到愛人所住的農場，整首詩就由這一連串的動作組成，非常的生動。

 詞藻釋義

☆ **beat** *v.* 打，擊，撲動，跳動
　　詩中指的心臟的跳動。

重點句型

複合形容詞

詩中的 sea-scented beach 是散發海水氣味的海灘，sea-scented 是一種複合形容詞，意思是兩個字組合而成的形容詞，中間要用連字號（hyphen）相連，常見的此類形容詞有 well-known、hard-working、English-speaking、mouth-watering、record-breaking、world-famous 等，組合的形式不一，有副詞加形容詞、名詞加動詞、名詞加形容詞等。

寫作指引

戀愛有各種不同的階段，從一開始的一見鍾情，中間經過約會，到最後的修成正果。

這封信是在說服女方接受約會的邀請，約會是戀愛必經的步驟，但有情調的約會要經過精心的設計和浪漫的安排，文字上的說服更是重要。

範例

You live in my heart. Every time I think of you, all I need to do is to look inside my heart to find you. I also hear in my heart a voice from you, which, though sweet and tender, makes my heart beat faster.

I aspire to meet you at a place, where our hearts can be in sync. I can find you and hear you in my heart, but I can't hear your heartbeat. That makes all the difference.

I know you have a place for me in your heart. But the relationship won't be complete if I can't hear your heartbeat and touch your heart.

With love.

中譯

　　妳活在我的心裡。每次一想到妳，我只要往心裡一瞧，就能找到妳，也能聽到妳的聲音，那是一種甜美溫柔的聲音，可是卻讓我的心跳加快。

　　我渴望與妳在一個我們的心可以一起跳動的地方相見。我能在我的心裡找到妳並聽到妳的聲音，可是卻聽不到妳的心跳，這是最大的差異。

　　我知道妳在妳的心裡有為我留一個位置，但這樣還不夠聽到我的心跳。

　　愛。

知識補給

　　英國維多利亞時期詩人暨劇作家羅伯特・布朗寧（1812-1889）擅長在詩中營造戲劇性獨白（dramatic monologue），這種文學形式最知名的例子是莎翁《哈姆雷特》劇作中的「存活下去抑或不」（To be, or not to be）獨白。布朗寧在《我的前公爵夫人》（My Last Duchess）中將這種文學形式發揮到淋漓盡致，但《相遇在夜晚》這首詩是另外一種形式，著重在用視覺及聽覺的意象營造出一種律動的感覺，從一開頭的海上看陸地，到最後兩人相見時女方發出比他們心跳聲還小的聲音，這是一個很妙的比喻，人發出的聲音竟然會比心跳聲還要小，這把整首詩帶到最高潮，也是愛侶最期盼的一刻。

Unit 16

倒裝句
威廉‧莎士比亞《你在那個時節可在我身上看到》（第 73 首 14 行詩）
William Shakespeare "That Time Of Year Thou Mayst In Me Behold (Sonnet 73)"

 **Classic 經典詩句**

> That time of year thou mayst in me behold
>
> When yellow leaves, or none, or few, do hang
>
> Upon those boughs which shake against the cold,
>
> Bare ruined choirs, where late the sweet birds sang.
>
> In me thou see'st the twilight of such day
>
> As after sunset fadeth in the west

　　《你在那個時節可在我身上看到》是莎士比亞 154 首 14 行詩中的第 73 首，和之前討論過的第 18 首不太一樣，是在感嘆青春的逝去，並強調這樣才要愛得更為強烈，以免來不及。其中著名的詩句為：That time of year thou mayst in me behold / When yellow leaves, or none, or few, do hang / Upon those boughs which shake against the cold, / Bare ruined choirs, where late the sweet birds sang.（你在那個時節可在我身上看到／寥寥無幾或完全

沒有黃葉／掛在寒風中擺盪的樹枝上／空蕩破敗的教堂裡再也聽不見鳥兒的歌唱）。本章節則要討論以下詩句內含的文法：In me thou see'st the twilight of such day / As after sunset fadeth in the west（在我身上你可看到暮靄／日落後向西邊緩緩消褪）。

　　詩中用入冬、白日將盡和黑夜來襲、及快要燃燒完的火焰等意象來表達青春和生命之將盡，此時有如隨風搖擺的枯枝殘葉、不再聽到唱詩班歌聲或鳥兒叫聲的殘破空蕩教堂裡、或是日薄西山前的殘光掠影。即便如此，詩人卻認為愛人可以愛得更為強烈，因為再不愛就來不及了。

☆ **bare** *adj.* 裸的，光禿禿的，空的
　　詩中指的是空無一物之意。

☆ **choir** *n.* 教堂的唱詩班
　　bare ruined choirs 是指殘破空蕩的教堂，choir 只是教堂中唱詩班所在之處，此時用來代替教堂，因為要和鳥兒的合唱相呼應。

重點句型

倒裝句

　　英文的倒裝句型通常是把要強調的部份放到句首，可以是否定的副詞（never、rarely、seldom、hardly、little、under no circumstances 等）、表示否定的副詞子句（not until 子句）、或表示方向或場所的副詞（片語）。

　　In me thou see'st the twilight of such day 這個句子運用到另外一種倒裝句型，也就是把 in me 擺到句首來強調在我身上這個概念，這種句型在詩的創作上很常見，但不常見於一般文章。

寫作指引

　　就算進入遲暮之年，也仍可以擁抱愛情，此時不是要愛到天長地久，而是把握時間好好地愛一場。

　　比較少人探討老年之愛，如何著手確實費思量。莎士比亞的這首詩剛好提供了靈感，當然之前探討過的葉慈的詩也頗有幫助。

範例

After all those years, you are still attractive to me. You might have wrinkles and lines on your face, which you don't seek to soften or remove through plastic surgery.

You might easily fall asleep as watching television. However, you still have your charming smile. You also keep your wit, which makes talks with you one of my greatest enjoyments.

Aging might be the biggest enemy to most women, but you seem to be an exception. You go grey in a graceful way and carry yourself in a dignified way. I just can't help but admire you the more.

With love.

中譯

　　經過那麼多年，妳仍然吸引著我。妳或許臉上有了皺紋和線條，但也不曾想用醫學美容將其除去。

　　妳或許會邊看電視邊打瞌睡。儘管如此，妳的笑容還是那麼迷人，妳也還保有機智，和妳聊天是我的最大的享受之一。

　　老化對大多數女人來說是最大的敵人，但妳似乎是例外。妳優雅地發出華髮，仍舊維持高貴的舉止。我不禁更加地愛慕起妳。

　　愛。

 知識補給

　　我們知道莎士比亞 154 首 14 行詩的前 126 首是獻給一位年輕的男子，這首也不例外，但詩人卻在感嘆自己已經老邁，不再讚美對方的青春容貌。情詩不見得要是年輕人對年輕人，中年人或老年人也有機會寫情詩。莎士比亞對英國文學的發展影響很大，首先是他創造出很多詞語或著名的句子，例如，常說的 All that glitters is not gold.（閃閃發光的東西不見得都是黃金）就出自《威尼斯商人》，Brave new world（美麗新世界）出自《暴風雨》，Brevity is the soul of wit.（簡潔是智慧的靈魂）則出自《哈姆雷特》。All's well that ends well 是《皆大歡喜》一劇的名稱，卻也成為英文的慣用語。

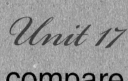

Unit 17

compare to / with
威廉・莎士比亞《我能否把你比為燦爛的夏日？》（第 18 首 14 行詩）
William Shakespeare "Shall I Compare Thee to a Summer's Day? (Sonnet 18)"

Shall I compare thee to a summer's day?

Thou art more lovely and more temperate.

Rough winds do shake the darling buds of May,

And summer's lease hath all too short a date.

　　英國大文豪威廉・莎士比亞（William Shakespeare）雖然以戲劇見長，但他的詩作也相當出色，尤其是 14 行詩。在他的 154 首 14 行詩中，又以第 18 首《我能否把你比為燦爛的夏日？》最有名，著名的詩句為：Shall I compare thee to a summer's day? / Thou art more lovely and more temperate. / Rough winds do shake the darling buds of May, / And summer's lease hath all too short a date.（我能否把你比為燦爛的夏日？／你比夏日更為可愛溫和／狂風摧殘五月時的嬌蕊／夏日來了卻又為時太短）。

 說文解詩

　　不說可能讀者不會注意到，這首詩的讚美對象是一個年輕男子，按照現在的眼光，可能會認為莎士比亞是一個同性戀，但是否如此並不妨礙這首詩成為英國最知名的情詩之一。莎翁用詞之精妙，著實令人讚嘆。例如，And every fair from fair sometime declines，精妙地說出每個美的事物的美都會衰減。

 詞藻釋義

☆ temperate　*adj.*　溫和的，不極端的

　　除了溫和之意外，還有節制的含義。詩中的意思應該是溫和的。

☆ lease　*n.*　租約，租契

　　直接把 summer's lease 翻成夏季的租期有點太直，其實就是指整個夏天，但由於夏天太短，感覺像是有租期。

重點句型

compare to / with

compare to 是將某人或某事物比為，可主動也可被動，主動形式句型為 compare＋受詞＋to，被動形式句型為 be compared to。

例如：I compare you to a summer's day.（我把你比為燦爛的夏日。）Nobody can be compared to Michael Jackson.（沒人能與麥可傑克森相比。）

類似的片語動詞 compare with 是比較的意思，有兩種用法，一種 compare A with B，另一種用法是 A compare with B。

例如，He compares himself physically with a friend of his.（他和他的一個朋友相比身材。）或 John's English compares poorly with Jack's.（約翰的英文沒有傑克好。）

寫作指引

用比喻方式來表達對某人的愛慕，通常會引用大家熟悉的事物，像是花草樹木，但比喻成夏天的例子算是很少見。

我們不是詩人，無法用不尋常的事物來做比喻，所以還是循規蹈矩用大家比較習慣的比喻，像是春天之類。

範例

You are like the spring, my love. I feel your presence with every breath I take and every soothing touch of the wind. You are everywhere. You are everything. I am but a receptacle of your love, passively receiving without giving something in return. I owe you so much.

You are also my inspiration. With you as my Muse, I have written several poems dedicated to people deeply in love. I will not compare you to a summer's day as Shakespeare did hundreds of years ago. The analogy is already a cliché. You deserve something new.

With love.

中譯

　　我的愛人，妳就像是春天。我每呼吸一次，每接觸到起著撫慰作用的春風時，都能感覺到妳的存在。妳是無所不在，妳是所有的一切。我只是接收妳的愛的容器，被動地在接收，卻沒能有所回饋。我欠妳太多了。

　　妳還是我的靈感源泉。有妳作為我的繆斯女神，我已經寫出一些獻給熱戀中男女的詩作。我不會像數百年前的莎士比亞一樣把妳比喻為夏天，這種比喻現在已是陳腔濫調，妳應該得到新的比喻。

　　愛。

 知識補給

　　威廉・莎士比亞（1564-1616）雖然現在被視為英國及全世界全傑出的作家之一，但當年卻成名比馬羅晚了許多，還從馬羅的幾齣戲劇取得創作的靈感。儘管如此，莎士比亞還是努力創作使自己達到文學的頂峰，一生總共創作出 38 部劇本和 154 首 14 行詩。在他的 154 首 14 行詩中，前 126 首是獻給一個稱為 fair youth 的年輕男子，第 127 首至最後一首則是獻給一位「黑女士」（dark lady）。有的評論家以前 126 首為證據認為莎士比亞是同性戀，雖然他已娶妻生子。但也有人認為莎士比亞只是為了修辭而修辭，不是真的在表達愛意，就這個觀點看來，莎翁似乎有點沈溺在他自己所創造的詩境而無法自拔。

Unit 18

somewhere
理查・拉加利安《詩歌：她在燦爛陽光中的某處》
Richard Le Gallienne "Song: 'She's somewhere in the sunlight strong'"

Classic 經典詩句

She's somewhere in the sunlight strong,

Her tears are in the falling rain,

She calls me in the wind's soft song,

And with the flowers she comes again.

　　英國現代詩人理查・拉加利安（Richard Le Gallienne）於 1916 年寫下這首《詩歌：她在燦爛陽光中的某處》，給人一種陽光燦爛的感覺，其中著名的詩句為：She's somewhere in the sunlight strong, / Her tears are in the falling rain, / She calls me in the wind's soft song, / And with the flowers she comes again.（她在燦爛陽光中的某處／她的眼淚在落下的雨中／她用風中的溫柔歌聲呼喚我／她隨著花兒再次來到）。

 說文解詩

　　這首短詩讚美愛人，把她比喻為燦爛陽光的一部份，天空落下的雨裡有她的眼淚，輕柔的風中傳來她的呼喚，她帶著繁花來到，遠方的鳥兒是她的信差，月亮是她銀色的座車，沒錯，太陽和月亮都是她派來的，還有靜靜在一旁待命的星星。

 詞藻釋義

☆ **somewhere** *adv.* 在某處，往某處，大概
　　somewhere about here 是就在這附近的意思。

somewhere

詩中用到 somewhere 這個字，意思是在某個未陳述或未知的地方。例如：

He lives somewhere in southern Taiwan.（他住在南臺灣某個地方。）

You must have put your book somewhere.（你一定把你的書放在某個地方。）

go somewhere 就是 go to some place 的意思。特別的是，somewhere 後面可以接不定詞。例如：

I am looking for somewhere to eat.（我在找地方吃飯。）

Let's find somewhere to hide and stay out of sight.（讓我們找個地方躲起來不讓人看到。）

另外，著名的電影《似曾相識》（Somewhere in Time）若是直譯，會翻成某個時間點，這樣就少了文字之美。

運用自然的意象來比喻女人之美，一直都是很好的策略，但也要有一定的文字功力才行。

運用玫瑰這個比喻來讚美愛人，同時也加入流行的花語，讓愛人在享受讚美之際也能學習各種花所代表的意義。

範例

As said in a poem, "My love is like a red, red rose."

I don't remember which poem. Be that as it may, I just want to emphasize that you are as beautiful as a rose, especially as you are in a red dress. A red rose symbolizes love. You are the embodiment of love.

You also look great as wearing a purple dress. A purple rose stands for grace and elegance.

I don't like you to wear a pink dress since that color seems to be only for kids or teenagers. You don't have to follow my advice if you don't like it.

With love.

中譯

如某首詩中所說：「我的愛人像是一朵紅紅的玫瑰」。

我不記得是哪首詩。不管怎樣，我只是想強調妳美得像朵玫瑰，尤其是當妳穿紅色衣服時。紅色玫瑰象徵愛情，妳就是愛情的化身。

妳穿紫色衣服也很好看，紫色衣服象徵優雅和典雅。

我不喜歡妳穿粉紅色衣服，因為那似乎是小孩或青少年在用的顏色。妳若不喜歡我的建議，就不用照著做。

愛。

 知識補給

　　理查‧拉加利安（1866-1947）除了是個詩人外，也從事過新聞工作，不過最早的工作是在會計師事務所，他在工作一段時間後改以作家為終生志業。出生於利物浦的拉加利安婚後曾經在美國和法國的不同城市住過，二次世界大戰期間為了躲避戰亂移居摩納哥，戰爭期間他拒絕為德國納粹或義大利政府寫宣傳文章，因而沒了收入，曾經餓到癱倒在街上。他有一個在美國當上電影和電視演員的女兒，她就是伊娃‧拉加利安（Eva Le Gallienne，1899–1991）。經歷過戰亂的拉加利安，寫過《上戰場的士兵》這首詩，他在詩中說：能把我的心一起帶著走／好讓我可以分享一點／你的知名事蹟？

Unit 19

so... that... / too...to...

亨利·沃茲沃思·朗費羅《箭與歌》

Henry Wadsworth Longfellow "The Arrow and the Song"

Classic 經典詩句

I shot an arrow into the air,

It fell to earth, I knew not where;

For, so swiftly it flew, the sight

Could not follow it in its flight.

...

For who has sight so keen and strong,

That it can follow the flight of song?

19 世紀美國詩人暨翻譯家亨利·沃茲沃思·朗費羅（Henry Wadsworth Longfellow）的詩作不但受到美國人喜愛，在國外也有很高的名氣，曾翻譯成多國語言，譬如中文。《箭與歌》的著名詩句為：I shot an arrow into the air, / It fell to earth, I knew not where; / For, so swiftly it flew, the sight / Could not follow it in its flight.（我把箭射入空中／箭落地後，我不知在哪裡／因為，它飛

行速度太快／眼睛追尋不到它的飛行路徑）。本章節則要討論以下詩句內含的文法：For who has sight so keen and strong, / That it can follow the flight of song?（誰的眼力如此尖，如此強／能追上歌聲飛揚？）。

 說文解詩

　　詩中的敘述者説他把箭射入空中後，看得到它落到地上，卻不知落在哪裡，因為箭的飛行速度快到肉眼無法追尋其飛行路徑。敘述者同時也哼出一首歌，歌曲也是在進入空中後不知去向，不過最後在一棵樹上找到射入的箭的同時，卻也發現消失的歌曲可以在朋友的心中找到。

詞藻釋義

☆ **swiftly** *adv.* 迅速地，敏捷地
act swiftly and decisively
迅速果決地行動

☆ **flight** *n.* 飛行
a long-distance flight
長途飛行

重點句型

so... that... / too... to

so... that 是太怎麼樣以至於怎麼樣的意思，可以和 too... to 相互替換。

例句：

It is so good that it can't be true.

等於 It is too good to be true.（這好得令人難以相信。）

The old man is so weak that he can't walk.

等於 The old man is too weak to walk.（老人虛弱到不能走路。）

The child is so young that he can't go to school.

等於 The child is too young to go to school.（小孩年紀小到不能去上學。）

寫作指引

把箭與歌曲做一對比，可發現相同與不同之處，愛情應該也能做類似的比喻。戀愛就像中了丘比特的箭一般，被射中的瞬間出現一種幸福感，如果同時也被她的歌聲打動，那可是效果加倍。

範例

As seeing you for the first time, I felt like being struck by Cupid's Arrow. It happened in a split second. I fell into euphoria.

The song you were singing at the time also greatly touched me. It struck my heart as fast as Cupid's Arrow. It did not give me a feeling of euphoria, however. It rather carried me away.

I sank into a state of intoxication because your voice was so beautiful. I can still hear the song in my heart despite a lapse of a few years.

You might not remember the song, and you did not know how I felt about your singing. What a bliss to hear you sing!

With love.

中譯

　　第一次看到妳時，我感覺中了愛神丘比特的箭。在那一瞬間，我墜入了幸福的狀態。

　　妳當時唱的那首歌也深深地打動我，它打動我心的速度和丘比特的箭一樣快，但給我的卻不是幸福感，而是讓我靈魂出竅。

　　妳的聲音是如此之美，以致於使我進入一種陶醉的狀態。儘管過了若干年，我仍可在心中聽到那首歌曲。

　　妳或許已不記得那首歌，且也不知道我對妳的唱歌的感受。能聽到妳唱歌真是一種福氣！

　　愛。

 知識補給

　　亨利・沃茲沃思・朗費羅（1807-1882）和許多美國詩人一樣都能用平易近人的文字和鮮明的比喻及意象來傳達一些人生的感受或哲理，很受一般美國人歡迎及接受，在國外也有相當的知名度。中國近代史上第一首翻譯自國外的英文詩就是朗費羅所寫的《人生頌》（A Psalm of Life），這是根據現代中國作家錢鐘書的考察，譯者則是清朝同治時期總理各國事務衙門全權大臣董恂，董恂不是第一個翻譯這首詩為中文的人，而是以原來的翻譯為本加以改進，並曾將《人生頌》書寫於扇子上轉交給遠在美國的朗費羅。在《箭與歌》這首詩中，朗費羅巧妙地把箭與歌做一並列對比，兩者同樣都是發出後就很快消失並不知去向，箭或許會停留在某個物體上，歌曲則會停留在聽到的人心中。

Unit 20
apart from
史派克·米尼根《祝你有個美好的一天》
Spike Milligan "Have A Nice Day"

 **Classic** 經典詩句

So the man who was drowning, drowned
And the man with the disease past away.
But apart from that,
And a fire in my flat,
It's been a very nice day.

　　當代愛爾蘭作家史派克·米尼根（Spike Milligan）用這首《祝你有個美好的一天》嘲諷人類的虛偽和愚蠢，其中著名的詩句為：So the man who was drowning, drowned / And the man with the disease past away. / But apart from that, / And a fire in my flat, / It's been a very nice day.（所以快要溺死的人溺死了／而生重病的人也死了／但除此之外／加上我屋子裡的爐火／算是一個美好的一天）。

　　這首詩比較像是一個短篇笑話，一個快要溺死在湖裡的人向岸上的另一個人求救，岸上的人卻說他生了重病，正在等他的醫生前來，要湖裡的人忍耐一下，因為醫生很快就會到。快要溺死的人竟也答應等待，結果這兩個人先後死去，誰也沒救到誰，讀者看了不免覺得荒謬和好笑。

☆ **drown** *v.* 淹死

fall in the water and drown

落水淹死

☆ **apart** *adv.* 相隔，相距

stand some distance apart

站離一段距離

apart from

詩中用到 apart from 這個介系詞片語，意思是除了…之外，等於 except，也就是不包括後面所接的名詞。

apart from 和 aside from 在意思和用法上相同，可表示除了…之外（except），也可表示除了…之外，還有（besides），要看上下文而定。例句：

Apart / Aside from the newcomer, all the others were there. （除了新人，其他人都在那裡。）

這個句子很明顯就是沒有包括後面所接的 newcomer。

Apart / Aside from being too large, the suit just doesn't suit me.（除了尺寸太大之外，這件襯衫就是不適合我。）

此時就有包括後面的意思。

文字是一項很有力的武器，可以用詼諧的方式來嘲諷人類的荒謬和愚蠢。

有些人過於理性，對何時談戀愛有預設的想法，但愛情說來就來，擋也擋不住，再多的理性分析也沒用。

範例

Have you been put in an absurd situation? What I mean by "absurd" is that the world often gives us things that we don't need as we want something else desperately.

In this sense, falling in love can be absurd sometimes. It may happen as you don't expect it to happen or don't want it to happen. It is true of our relationship.

As I met you for the first time, I was not ready for a relationship. Your beauty struck deep into my heart, prompting me to forget about my "absurd" situation and go for it.

With love.

中譯

　　妳曾碰過荒謬的處境嗎？所謂「荒謬」是指這個世界經常在我們急需某樣東西的時候給我們另一樣東西。

　　按照這個意義，愛上某人有時也是一種荒謬的發生，因為發生之時可能是你並不期待或不想有愛情的時候。我們的關係也是這樣。

　　當我第一次見到妳時，我沒準備要發展一段戀情。妳的美卻深深打動我的心，使我忘了「荒謬的」處境，勇敢去爭取。

　　愛。

 知識補給

　　史派克・米尼根（1918-2002）除了是作家外，還是喜劇演員。他的許多詩作被歸類為胡說八道詩（nonsense poetry），其中一首詩曾在 1998 年的全英國票選中被選為最受喜歡的搞笑詩，勝過胡說八道詩派的代表性人物路易斯・卡羅和愛德華・李爾。胡說八道詩也不是真的在胡說八道，而是用散文的形式和幽默的口吻來表達一些枯燥乏味的事理，就像《祝你有個美好的一天》是用一個可笑的故事來嘲諷的人類愚蠢。在正常的況狀下，快要在湖裡溺死的人向岸上的人求救，應該得到正面的回應才對，可是沒想到可以救他的人卻患了重病，無法救他。岸上的人要溺水者稍安勿躁，因為他的醫師就快來了，兩人就一起等，最後一起死去。

Part 2

愛的恐懼與不安

Unit 1
從屬子句
克勞德‧麥凱《如果我們必須死去》
Claude McKay "If We Must Die"

Classic 經典詩句

If we must die, let it not be like hogs

Hunted and penned in an inglorious spot,

While round us bark the mad and hungry dogs,

Making their mock at our accursèd lot.

If we must die, O let us nobly die,

So that our precious blood may not be shed in vain

　　20 世紀牙買加裔美籍作家克勞德‧麥凱（Claude McKay）較為出名的作品是他的小說，這首《如果我們必須死去》是在表達非裔美人對當年美國種族主義的反抗，著名的詩句為：If we must die, let it not be like hogs / Hunted and penned in an inglorious spot, / While round us bark the mad and hungry dogs, / Making their mock at our accursèd lot.（如果我們必須死去，不要讓我們像豬一樣／被追捕並被圍在不光彩的地方／周圍盡是對我們咆哮的發瘋餓狗／

牠們在嘲笑我們受到詛咒的命運）。本章節則要討論以下詩句內含的文法：If we must die, O let us nobly die, / So that our precious blood may not be shed in vain（如果我們必須死去，噢讓我們光榮地死去／這樣我們珍貴的鮮血就不至於白流）。）。

說文解詩

　　這首詩是針對 1919 年的紅色夏季暴動事件而作，當時美國各地發生種族暴動，主要是白人攻擊黑人事件，許多黑人起而反抗，特別是在芝加哥和華盛頓特區等地。詩人在詩中說，如果我們必須死去，就讓我們光榮地死去，不要讓我們的鮮血白流。

詞藻釋義

☆ hog　*n.*　豬；【美】長大的食用豬

　　常說的 eat like a hog 就是吃得像豬一樣。

☆ pen　*v.*　把（家畜）關入圍欄；把……關起來

　　通常是指把家畜關在圍欄裡，詩中隱喻為把人當成畜生一樣圍起來。

☆ lot　*n.*　命運，運氣

　　在詩人創作的年代，這個詞是命運之意，相當於 luck。

重點句型

從屬子句

詩中用到 so that 句型，這是一種表達目的的從屬子句，等於 in order that、so as to 及 in order to。

例句：我為了搭到公車早起。

I got up early so that I could catch the bus.

I got up early in order that I could catch the bus.

I got up early in order to catch the bus.

I got up early so as to catch the bus.

但 in order that 和 in order to 可以擺到句首加強語氣，so that 和 so as to 不行。不要把 so that 句型和 so...that 句型搞混，後者是太怎樣而怎樣的意思，例如：He is so clever that he can answer the question. （他是如此聰明，所以能回答問題。）

寫作指引

戀愛有時會碰上時代的動亂或戰事，處此當下，戀人該如何自處？

戀愛有酸甜苦辣，有好日子也有壞日子，碰上好日子就順著過，碰上壞日子也要過，相互鼓勵很重要，讓雙方對未來抱持信心。

範例

As hard times befall on us, we have only each other to count on. Whatever may happen, you can always find me somewhere near your place.

As German philosopher Hegel has said, people and governments never have learned anything from history. They are making the same foolish mistakes as those people did hundreds of years ago. Their mistakes have made our lives miserable. We have no choice but to live through the bad days.

Don't lose faith in life. I'll be by your side. You can come to me if you want. I have already prepared for your visit.

With love.

1
Part

2
Part

3
Part

中譯

　　當我們遭遇到艱難時刻，我們只有彼此可以依靠。不管發生什麼事情，妳總是能在妳的附近找到我。

　　如德國哲學家黑格爾所說，人們和政府從未曾從歷史學到教訓，他們所犯的錯誤讓我們的生活變得難過，我們別無選擇只能設法熬過這些苦日子。

　　不要對生命喪失信心，我會在妳的身邊。妳如果想要可以來到我這邊，我已為妳的到來做好準備。

　　愛。

知識補給

　　克勞德‧麥凱（1889-1948）在《如果我們必須死去》中表現出對同種族人民的大愛，他特地寫下這首詩來表達對種族主義的不滿。他是紐約哈林文藝復興運動（Harlem Renaissance）的重要人物，該運動的目的主要是在反種族歧視，鼓勵黑人作家從事文藝創作並歌頌黑人精神。麥凱 1928 出版的小説《回到哈林》（Home to Harlem）是他最知名的作品，內容描寫哈林區的街頭生活，對加勒比海地區、西非、及歐洲等地的黑人知識份子產生很大的影響。這本小説讓他贏得一項文學獎項。在《如果我們必須死去》中，麥凱鼓吹黑人同胞起來反抗，儘管可能會死亡，但也要死得光榮，讓敵人不得不尊重我們。雖然現在的時空環境已大不相同，但我們還是要學習如何用大愛來包容不同的族裔。

Unit 2
介系詞 in spite of
莎拉‧蒂斯戴爾《寂寞》
Sara Teasdale "Alone"

Classic 經典詩句

I am alone, in spite of love,

In spite of all I take and give—

In spite of all your tenderness,

Sometimes I am not glad to live.

20 世紀美國人女詩人莎拉‧蒂斯戴爾（Sara Teasdale）在這首《寂寞》中表達出寂寞孤寂之情，著名詩句為：I am alone, in spite of love, / In spite of all I take and give— / In spite of all your tenderness, / Sometimes I am not glad to live（我獨自一人，儘管有愛／儘管我的付出與給予——／儘管你全然的溫柔／有時我活著並不快樂）。

說文解詩

　　詩人用這首詩來表達寂寞孤寂之情，這是英詩中的傳統主題之一，就是在表達一種愁思（melancholy），這從現代的角度來看可能是一種憂鬱症（melancholia），但以前人不知道那是一種疾病，用詩詞來抒發內心鬱悶也是一種治療方式。

詞藻釋義

☆ alone　*adj.*　單獨的，獨自的

　　通常是指獨自一人，不見得是孤單（lonely），要注意 alone 和 lonely 之間意思上的差別，但在這首詩中，alone 偏向孤單之意。

☆ tenderness　*n.*　溫柔

　　除了溫柔之意外，也相當於愛（love）。

介系詞 *in spite of*

　　這首詩中用到 in spite of（雖然，儘管）這個介系詞，它可與 despite、for all、with all 等意義相同的介系詞相互替換，表達一種詞意上的轉折，後面是接名詞或動名詞。

　　例句：儘管生病，約翰還是去學校。

Despite his illness, John went to school.

Despite the fact that he was ill, John went to school.

Despite being ill, John went to school

Although he was ill, John went to school.

　　這幾個句子的意思都相同，只是用不同的句型來表達罷了。這些表達意義上轉折的介系詞可擺在句首或句尾，但擺在句首的機率似乎較高。

寫作指引

　　戀愛時有各種的滋味，酸甜苦辣都有，不會只有甜蜜的感覺，苦澀的感覺有時也要體會一下。

　　以下的例子：男方有事要出差幾天，可是女方大小事都依賴他，所以一方面要安撫她，另一方面則要幫她把事情處理好，不然她可會不高興。

範例

It is not easy to be alone. I know you need me to be with you. But I have things to do. I have to go on a business trip for my company.

I'll be away for just a few days. I know you are in the habit of having me run errands for you. Old habits die hard, so to speak. With that in mind, I have already made arrangements for you in advance. Don't worry that I might leave things undone.

You are everything to me. Whatever might happen, I'll never leave you in a state of helplessness.

With love.

Part 1

Part 2

Part 3

中譯

　　獨自一人並不容易。我知道妳需要我在妳身邊，可是我有事要做，要為公司出一趟差。

　　我只會離開幾天，我知道妳已經養成讓我幫妳處理雜事的習慣，正所謂舊習難改。我有考慮到這一點，所以事先幫妳做好安排，不要擔心我會有事情沒做。

　　妳是我的一切，不管怎樣，我都不會讓妳陷入無助的境地。

　　愛。

知識補給

　　莎拉·蒂斯戴爾（1884-1933）為美國近代抒情詩人，出生於美國密蘇里州聖路易斯市，從《寂寞》這首詩或許可看出她相當多愁善感，許多文學家都有這種特質，但有些作家能從作品中抽離出來，有些則不能，終至深陷自己所營造的情境之中。蒂斯戴爾於 1933 年因服用過量安眠藥而身亡。她於 1918 年因其詩作上的表現而獲得普立茲獎的肯定，她的婚姻生活不算美滿，因為經商的先生經常出差在外，她的詩作或許剛好反應出她內心的孤寂，儘管在物質生活上並不匱乏。在《寂寞》這首詩中，詩人說：我獨自一人，好像站在一個疲憊灰色世界的頂峰，周圍只見盤旋不斷的白雪，往上看則是無窮無盡的宇宙。

1
Part

2
Part

3
Part

Unit 3
祈使句
馬修・阿諾德《多佛海灘》
Matthew Arnold "Dover Beach"

 **Classic 經典詩句**

Ah, love, let us be true

To one another! for the world, which seems

To lie before us like a land of dreams

　　英國維多利亞時期詩人馬修・阿諾德（Matthew Arnold）1867年出版的《多佛海灘》是他最著名的詩作之一，其中最為大家熟知的詩句為 Ah, love, let us be true / To one another! for the world, which seems / To lie before us like a land of dreams（我的愛啊！讓我們忠於／彼此，因為這個世界似乎／如夢境般展現在我們的面前）。

 說文解詩

　　既是詩人也是評論家的阿諾德，在這首詩中藉由觀海來表達身處不確定年代及新舊交替之際所感受的哀愁，唯一可確定的是他與愛人彼此忠誠，共同面對一個看似夢境的世界。那是一個有著許多變化的美麗新世界，卻少了快樂、愛和光明。

 詞藻釋義

☆ **be true to** 忠實於

　　詩中的 let us be true to one another，就是讓我們忠於彼此的意思，按照現在的文法，如果只牽涉到兩個人，該用 each other 而不是 one another，不過早期的文法和現在的不一樣。

祈使句

　　在 Ah, love, let us be true / To one another!這兩行詩句中，我們看到 let（允許，讓）這個祈使語氣動詞，它是及物動詞，後面接受詞，再接原形動詞，被動式時要在動詞的過去分詞前加 be 動詞。例如：Let us pray.（讓我們祈禱。）是正式的說法，但現在許多人喜歡非正式說法，即 Let's pray.不過前提是受詞必須為第一人稱複數 we 的受格 us。

　　這首詩的創作年代應該還沒有非正式的 let's 說法，所以 let us be true 無法改成 let's be true，況且改了會改變原有的音步（foot）。

　　這首詩帶出一種面臨時代改變時的懷舊之情和不安之心，我們寫作時或可做一參考。

　　碰到時代的變遷，愛情也會受到考驗，尤其是一方有很多事要處理時，此時另一方就要信任對方，給對方處理的時間，如此才能共同克服困難。

範例

1 Part

2 Part

3 Part

Whatever may happen, we must be true to each other.

You are always on my mind. The world is changing at a rapid pace. Be that as it may, my love for you will be the same, as solid as a rock.

Who loves you the most? Love conquers all. Don't fear the obstacles that lie ahead. As long as we have confidence, we can make it.

I have things to take care of recently, so I have no choice but to leave you unattended for quite a while. Please trust me. Trust is an essential part of love.

With love.

中譯

不管發生什麼事，我們必須真誠相待。

我總是想到妳。世界正在快速地轉變，儘管如此，我對妳的愛還是一樣，堅如磐石。

誰最愛妳？愛能征服一切，不要怕前方的障礙，只要我們有信心，就能達成目標。

最近我有一些事情要處理，所以不得不讓妳沒人陪有好一陣子。請信任我，信任是愛不可或缺的一部份。

愛。

知識補給

　　馬修‧阿諾德（1822-1888）身處在快速變化的維多利亞時期，此一時期出現了大英帝國擴張、工業革命、達爾文進化論等巨大的變化，面對時代巨變的阿諾德用《多佛海灘》來表達內心的複雜情緒，尤其是對宗教信仰的衰退更有很大的感觸，原本的信仰之海（The Sea of Faith）曾經是滿潮並環繞世界各地的海岸（Was once, too, at the full, and round earth's shore），可是現在只能聽到它的哀怨之聲及退潮時拉長的嗚咽聲（Its melancholy, long, withdrawing roar）。詩中提到了古希臘劇作家索福克勒斯（Sophocles），他最著名的作品為《伊底帕斯王》，詩人提到他的目的是說當年索福克勒斯也在愛琴海邊聽見這種潮起潮落的聲音，就和他在多佛海邊聽到的一樣。

Unit 4

主詞＋受詞＋受詞補語
瑪格麗特・伊莉莎白・單斯特《遺漏的罪惡》

Margaret Elizabeth Sangster, "The Sin of Omission"

 **Classic** 經典詩句

It isn't the thing you do, dear;
It's the thing you leave undone,
Which gives you a bit of heartache
At the setting of the sun.

19 世紀末至 20 世紀初美國女詩人瑪格麗特・伊莉莎白・單斯特（Margaret Elizabeth Sangster）出身基督教家庭，似乎在這首《遺漏的罪惡》中傳達出一種具有責任感的愛。著名的詩句為：It isn't the thing you do, dear; / It's the thing you leave undone, / Which gives you a bit of heartache / At the setting of the sun.（不是你做了的事，親愛的／而是你沒做的事／會讓你有點心痛／在黃昏時刻）。

 說文解詩

　　現代一般人比較不會覺得沒做完一件事或忘了做某件事是一個罪惡，但在單斯特那個年代及那樣的家庭背景下，恐怕不是一件可以輕忽的不好習慣。如果你送了花過去，卻忘了隨附一封充滿愛語的信，到頭來反而會成為你自己的夢魘。

 詞藻釋義

☆ undone　*adj.*　未做的，未完成的
leave one's work undone
丟下工作不管

☆ heartache　*n.*　心痛
類似的詞語有 headache（頭痛）、stomachache（胃痛）等。

重點句型

主詞＋受詞＋受詞補語

詩中的 leave something undone 的句型是英文五大句型中的主詞＋受詞＋受詞補語（現在分詞、過去分詞或形容詞），常見的 leave someone alone 也是這類句型。

keep 和 leave 是這類句型常用到的動詞，如：You must keep your room clean.

另外，make、find 及 have 等動詞也適用這類句型，不過用法和 keep 及 leave 不太一樣，要特別注意。

寫作指引

做了許多好事，卻忘了其中關鍵事項，結果反而成為重大的遺憾。

常常見到人到了卻忘了帶某樣東西這種狀況，儘管不是故意的，還是要道歉並做補救動作，這樣才能讓愛人滿意。

範例

I have to apologize to you for having forgotten to bring you the gift that I promised to give you. I just thought of going to your place as soon as possible, but haste makes waste.

What's worse, I was caught in a traffic jam. I got angry at the traffic jam. It drove me crazy.

As my taxi finally reached the stop near your house, I was in such a rush that I left the gift for you in the cab. How foolish I was!

I promise not to make the same mistake again. At least I arrived in person to celebrate your birthday.

With love.

1
Part

2
Part

3
Part

中譯

對於未能帶給妳我原先承諾給妳的禮物，我必須道歉。我當時只想到盡快到妳那裡，但欲速則不達。

更糟的是，我陷入到塞車陣中，並為此發了脾氣，車子塞到讓我發狂。

當我搭的計程車抵達妳家附近的招呼站時，我趕忙下車卻把忘了把禮物帶下車，實在有夠愚蠢！

我向妳保證不會再犯這種錯誤。我上次至少親自到場慶祝妳的生日。

愛。

知識補給

　　美國女詩人瑪格麗特・伊莉莎白・單斯特（1838-1912）除了寫詩外，也寫散文，並擔任過著名 Harper's Bazaar 雜誌的編輯。她經由作品結識了當時著名的人物，如大文豪馬克吐溫和知名殘障作家海倫・凱勒。17 歲就開始寫作的她寫了不少給兒童閱讀的散文作品。在這首《遺漏的罪惡》中，單斯特傳達出一種及時行善和勿掛一漏萬的訊息，一件做了 90%的好事，可能會因為剩下沒做的 10%給搞砸，況且這些事都不是什麼難事，只是一些小小的善行（little acts of kindness），話雖如此，這些小小的行為卻是讓你可能成為天使的機會（Those chances to be angels），何樂而不為？我們的生命是如此短暫，悲哀的事卻又如此之大。

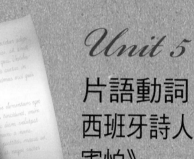

Unit 5

片語動詞 be afraid of
西班牙詩人雷蒙・甘布亞摩《兩種害怕》——班・卡魯瑟斯英譯
Spanish poet Ramon de Campoamor
"Two Fears" ——translated by Ben
Carruthers

Classic 經典詩句

When night fell on that lovely day

she, removed from me,

asked, "Why do you draw so near?

I am afraid of you!"

　　19 世紀西班牙詩人暨哲學家雷蒙・甘布亞摩（Ramon de Campoamor）雖然不是用英文創作，但從這首《兩種害怕》的英文版本也可看出不少趣味，拉丁民族對愛的看法還是和説英語的盎格魯撒克遜人略有不同，詩中著名的詩句為：When night fell on that lovely day / she, removed from me, / asked, "Why do you draw so near? / I am afraid of you!"（當那個美好一天的夜晚降臨時／她坐離我遠一點／還問，「你為什麼這麼靠近我？／我怕你！」）。

 說文解詩

　　所謂兩種害怕，就是女人一方面怕男人靠太近，另一方面卻又怕男人沒有靠太近，不在自己的身邊。這相當於中文裡的欲拒還迎，但也不完全等於，因為詩的一開頭就點出夜晚的降臨，此時女方或許擔心發生性關係，所以保持距離，等到夜晚過去後，她才又要男子靠近，這也算是一種合理的自我保護。

 詞藻釋義

☆ **removed** *adj.* 遠離的，離開的

　　從 remove 動詞的過去分詞變來的形容詞，後面要接 from。

☆ **draw** *v.* 移動，來到

Draw near, please.

請靠近。

重點句型

片語動詞 *be afraid of*

詩中用到 be afraid of 這個片語動詞，意思是害怕，be afraid to 也有類似的意思，但不完全一樣，首先，前者的 of 後面要接動名詞，後者則是接不定詞，這是第一個不同之處。

其次，be afraid of doing something 表示不敢或不情願做某件事，但不見得能不去做，如 He is afraid of being scolded by his father because of his poor grades in school. 而 be afraid to 則表示不敢去做某件事且可以不去做，如 She is afraid to go out alone at night.

寫作指引

女人經常出現矛盾的心理，明明喜歡你，卻又保持一段距離，這就是所謂的矜持。

用實際的案例來説明女人的矛盾心理，男方一開始不懂怎麼一回事，事後讀了一些書才懂，所以讀書還是挺有用的。

範例

Remember the night we went out together to enjoy the night scenery of Taipei? You were excited and passionate at first, but you later became subdued and not responsive to my sweet words.

I didn't know what happened. Did I offend you in one way or another? Not that I could remember.

After the episode, I read some books to find out why. You were just being coy with me. With that understanding, I am now more capable of responding properly to the subtle feeling of a woman. There is no need to be shy with me.

With love.

中譯

　　還記得我們一起外出看台北夜景的那個夜晚？妳一開始很興奮熱情，可是過了一會就變得收斂，對我的甜言蜜語毫無反應。

　　我不知道怎麼回事。有哪些地方冒犯到妳嗎？我不記得有。

　　經過那次經驗後，我看了一些書才找到答案，原來妳只是害羞。有了這個瞭解之後，我對女人的細膩感情比較能夠做出適當的反應。沒必要跟我害羞。

　　愛。

知識補給

　　西班牙詩人雷蒙‧甘布亞摩（1817-1901）也是一位哲學家，創作年代正值西班牙浪漫主義時期，他剛開始也是往浪漫主義風格發展，但不太成功，於是改寫一種類似打油詩的詼諧幽默寫法，沒想到反而受到歡迎，這首《兩種害怕》某種程度上反映出這種傾向，簡單來說，就是用詼諧幽默的方式把簡單的人生道理講述出來，甘布亞摩因此也被稱為哲學詩人。有趣的是，甘布亞摩原先想要進入耶穌會傳道，沒想到後來會成為一個詩人。從《兩種害怕》可看出他對性愛的保守態度，這在 19 世紀的歐洲應該是一種主流思想，但隨著時代的改變，這首短詩卻不顯得古板，因為裡面蘊藏了極大的幽默感。

Unit 6
不定詞作形容詞用
查爾斯・狄更斯《露西之歌》
Charles Dickens "Lucy's Song in The Village Coquettes"

Classic 經典詩句

Love is not a feeling to pass away,

Like the balmy breath of a summer day;

It is not— it cannot be— laid aside;

It is not a thing to forget or hide.

19 世紀英國大文豪查爾斯・狄更斯（Charles Dickens）在《風騷村姑》（The Village Coquettes）音樂劇中加入這首《露西之歌》，成為以小說創作為主的他少數的詩歌作品，其中著名的詩句為：Love is not a feeling to pass away, / Like the balmy breath of a summer day; / It is not — it cannot be — laid aside; / It is not a thing to forget or hide.（愛不是會消逝的感情／像是夏日的微風一般／它不被一也不能一棄置一旁／它不是可以忘記或隱藏的東西）。

 說文解詩

　　愛是一種不會消逝的感情，就像是夏日微風一般，不會被棄置一旁，也不會被忘記或隱藏。它緊緊地依附在心上，就像常春藤依附在榆樹上一般。愛不是一種追求榮耀、名聲或金子的渴望，在這些渴望消失之後，愛仍持續存在，且更有力量。

 詞藻釋義

☆ **balmy** *adj.* 芳香的，溫和的

　balmy air 溫和的空氣

☆ **lay aside** 儲藏，拋棄，革除，棄置

重點句型

不定詞作形容詞用

之前的單元討論過不定詞片語，不定詞片語可以作為名詞、形容詞或副詞用，副詞功能部分已討論過，不再重複。

這裡要討論的是不定詞的形容詞用法，詩中的 a feeling to pass away 和 a thing to forget or hide 都用不定詞片語來修飾前面的名詞。

例句：

He needs some water to drink.（to drink 是在修飾 water）

We have something to do.（to do 是在修飾 something）

不定詞片語裡的動詞是要能對所修飾名詞做出動作的動詞才行，如 some water to drink 在意義上等同於 drink some water。

寫作指引

愛是永恆也無所不在，無法將其隱藏或遺忘，因為它就像蔓藤一樣依附在心上。

戀愛時如果愛人喜歡從事某些事情，不妨一起去做，這樣不但能增進感情，也能散播正面的能量，讓周遭的人都能感受到。

範例

Love is everywhere. You can feel and find it everywhere you go. You don't need to love everyone, but you can spread love to everyone.

As you spread love, you also spread joy. I myself feel the power of your love. It is not just love between a man and a woman. It is love for all people. Your love influences me in a positive way. I now feel an urge to spread love as far and as wide as I can.

With you as my model, I have become a volunteer for a charity organization. I have to thank you for that.

With love.

中譯

　　愛無所不在，不管你走到哪都能發現並感受到它。你不必愛上每個人，可是你可以把愛傳播給每個人。

　　當你散播愛時，也在傳播歡樂，我自己感受到妳的愛，那不只是男人與女人之間的愛，而是對大眾的愛。妳的愛對我有正面的影響，我現在感到一股想把愛傳播出去的衝動，能傳多遠就多遠，能傳多廣就多廣。

　　有妳作為我的榜樣，我現在已成為某個慈善團體的志工，我必須感謝妳給我的影響。

　　愛。

知識補給

　　查爾斯・狄更斯（1812-1870）是英國維多利亞時期最偉大的作家，創作出一些對後世產生很大影響的小説，像是《孤雛淚》、《小氣財神》、《塊肉餘生錄》、《艱難時代》、《雙城記》等。他之所以偉大，主要是他生動地描寫出當時社會的實際景況，更在小説中塑造出一些代表性的人物，讓讀者看了之後很難忘記，像是《小氣財神》（或譯《聖誕頌歌》）中的守財奴史古基，狄更斯在小説人物身上注入大家或多或少都有的特質，讓人讀了除了感到強烈的吸引力外，還有心有戚戚焉之感。狄更斯另一偉大之處是他不但創作量驚人，且幾乎每本小説都相當受到歡迎及好評。古往今來沒幾人能有這樣的成就和地位。

Unit 7
不定代名詞
華萊士・史蒂文斯《雪人》
Wallace Stevens "The Snow Man"

Classic 經典詩句

One must have a mind of winter

To regard the frost and the boughs

Of the pine-trees crusted with snow.

...

For the listener, who listens in the snow,

And, nothing himself, beholds

Nothing that is not there and the nothing that is.

20 世紀美國大詩人華萊士・史蒂文斯（Wallace Stevens）在《雪人》中用雪景表達出一種深遠的意境，著名的詩句為：For the listener, who listens in the snow, / And, nothing himself, beholds / Nothing that is not there and the nothing that is.（對在雪中聆聽的聆聽者來說／本是空無的他看著／不存在的空無和存在的空無）。本章節則要討論以下詩句內含的文法：One must have a

mind of winter / To regard the frost and the boughs / Of the pine-trees crusted with snow.（人要有冬天之心／以察覺感知霜雪松枝）。

 說文解詩

詩人一開頭就說人要有冬天之心（a mind of winter）才能注意到覆滿積雪松樹上結霜的樹枝，也就是感同身受，但雪地中的雪人，由於本身就是虛無，故能看到不存在的虛無和存在的虛無。兩相比較，感同身受固然好，但也是一種影響客觀視野的主觀情感。

 詞藻釋義

☆ **behold** *v.* 觀看，注視，觀察

經常用在祈使語句，表達「看哪！」之意。

☆ **nothing** *n.* 沒有，沒有什麼東西，無，空，不存在

詩中用 nothing 來表達一種哲學上的空無，或是虛無。

不定代名詞

詩中提到One must have a mind of winter，one 是一種不定代名詞，表示任何一個人，其他不定代名詞如 some 和 any 也在表達不特定的一些人或個人。

例句：
One can't be too careful.（再小心也不為過。）

由於泛指任何一個人，所以 one 也可用 you 代替，翻譯時就不用把一個人或你翻出來。one 和 you 可相互替換，但 one 用在比較正式的語句，表達一般性的事物或道理，如做事要小心之類。例句：
One / You should knock before going into somebody's room.

這首詩讓我們知道設身處地為人著想的必要性，如此才能真正了解對方。

男女交往總有一方要讓步，儘管男方不喜歡女方購物，但也不好反對，只能從中找到樂趣和好處，那就是和女方相處的時間變多了。

範例

Sometimes I wonder whether I really understand you. Maybe it is because I have never put myself in your position. That's the problem.

You like to go shopping, while I feel bored at the same time. Could we do something else? Every time you go on a shopping spree, I am bored out of my mind. What is the fun of shopping?

For me, the greatest pleasure in going shopping with you is that I can be with you. Being bored in the meantime is not so much undesirable, after all. Being with you makes me happy. That's all I care about.

With love.

中譯

　　有時我不知道是否真的了解妳，或許是因為我從未設身處地為妳想過，那是問題的所在。

　　妳喜歡逛街購物，我則感到很無聊。我們可以做些別的事嗎？每次妳跑去瘋狂採購，我就覺得很無聊。購物的樂趣何在？

　　對我來說，和妳一起逛街購物的最大樂趣是在於能和妳在一起。期間感到無聊並不是那麼不好，和妳在一起讓我感到快樂，我只在乎這些。

　　愛。

知識補給

　　華萊士・史蒂文斯（1879-1955）為美國現代主義派（Modernist）詩人，1955 年曾獲得普立茲文學獎。雖然是個傑出的大詩人，史蒂文斯一生大部分時間都在康乃迪克州一間保險公司擔任高級主管，也曾在紐約市一家律師事務所工作過。所以不是學文學出身的他，通常利用閒暇時間在辦公室從事創作，寫出一些傳頌至今的絕好詩作。史蒂文斯的詩作受到英國浪漫主義和法國象徵主義的影響，所營造的意象更融入印象派（Impressionist）畫派的風格。更重要的是，他在詩中表達出一種美的哲學，透過想像力的運用來營造出一種現實，《雪人》最終想呈現的是類似佛教禪宗所說的「本來無一物，何處惹塵埃」境界。

Unit 8

be filled with / be full of

保羅・勞倫斯・鄧巴《光輝燦爛的一天》

Paul Laurence Dunbar "A Golden Day"

Classic 經典詩句

I found you and I lost you,

All on a gleaming day,

The day was filled with sunshine,

And the land was full of May.

美國非裔詩人保羅・勞倫斯・鄧巴（Paul Laurence Dunbar）在《光輝燦爛的一天》中用燦爛的一天來串連得與失，著名的詩句為：I found you and I lost you, / All on a gleaming day, / The day was filled with sunshine, / And the land was full of May.（我找到妳和失去妳／都在光輝燦爛的一天／那是個充滿陽光的日子／大地滿溢著五月的氣息）。

說文解詩

　　詩人說他找到和失去愛人都在一個陽光燦爛的日子（on a gleaming day），那是一個充滿陽光的日子（The day was filled with sunshine），大地則充滿了五月的氣息，這是一個光輝燦爛的日子，就算失去妳，只要夢到妳，就會憶起那五月的氣息。

詞藻釋義

☆ **golden** *adj.* 金色的，寶貴的，隆盛的
a golden opportunity
千載難逢的機會

☆ **brim** *v.* 裝滿，注滿
brim a glass with wine
斟滿一杯酒

be filled with / be full of

詩中用到 be filled with 和 be full of 這兩個意思類似的動詞片語，都有「裝滿」或「充滿」之意，但還是有些不同。前者表示裝得滿滿的，不留下任何空間，後者表示一種滿滿的感覺，不是真的滿到沒有任何空間。

例句：銀行下午通常都擠滿人。

The bank is usually filled with people in the afternoon.

The bank is usually full of people in the afternoon.

這兩個句子何者為對？

答案是後者。通常不會用前一個句子來描述某個空間擠滿了人的狀況。

對等連接詞 and 通常連接兩個意義類似的概念，可是在 I found you and I lost you 中卻用 and 連結看似相反的概念，形成一種反差。

經常關心女友是必要的，但有時會詞窮，所以多讀一點古典作品也是有用的，把女友比喻成特洛伊戰爭中的海倫，哪個女人看了不心花怒放？

範例

A shiny day is a golden day. And everyday can be a golden day as long as I think of your smile.

Your smile shines a light upon me, making my heart brim with joy. Is there a more heart-warming smile in the world? As Helen of Troy in ancient times, you have a face that can sink a thousand ships. That's enough to make my life shine.

As time goes by, all that remains unchanged is the look of you in my mind. As long as I dream of you, everyday can be a golden day.

With love.

中譯

　　天氣晴朗的一天就是燦爛的一天。只要我想到妳，每天都可以是燦爛的一天。

　　妳的笑容照亮了我，讓我的心充滿喜悅。這世上有更溫暖人心的笑容嗎？如同古代特洛伊城的海倫一般，妳擁有一張可以使一千艘戰船沈沒的容顏，這樣就足以使我的生命發亮起來。

　　隨著時間過去，不變的是妳在我心中的樣子。只要我夢到妳，每天都可以是燦爛的一天。

　　愛。

知識補給

　　保羅・羅倫斯・鄧巴（1872-1906）是美國第一位獲得全國肯定的非裔詩人。他的父母是肯塔基州獲得解放的黑奴，他們在白人農場的生活經歷形成保羅創作時的題材來源。鄧巴很早顯露詩才，14 歲就出版詩作，可惜由於財務困難無法上大學，只能擔任電梯操作員維持生計。他在 1893 年自費出版詩集，為了支付出版的費用，還向搭乘電梯的乘客以一本一美元的價格兜售他的詩集。在朋友的幫助下，他的詩作逐漸出現在全美主要的報紙和雜誌上，其中包括著名的《紐約時報》。鄧巴之後數年成為全國知名的作家，但不幸英年早逝，死時才 34 歲。除了詩作外，鄧巴也創作小說和短篇小說。

Unit 9
be 動詞+形容詞+of
詹姆士‧羅素‧羅威爾《噴水池》
James Russell Lowell "The Fountain"

Classic 經典詩句

Full of a nature

Nothing can tame,

Changed every moment,

Ever the same;—

美國詩人詹姆士‧羅素‧羅威爾（James Russell Lowell）在《噴水池》中用噴水池來表達一種變動中的不變，著名的詩句為：Full of a nature / Nothing can tame, / Changed every moment, / Ever the same（充滿了一種特質／沒有事物可以馴服／每一分鐘都在改變／卻總是一樣）。

 說文解詩

　　詩人讚美噴水池在不同時間的風貌，有日光下的風貌，有月光下的風貌，也有星光下的風貌。噴水池在不同時刻展現不同的風貌，不斷在流動，也不斷在變化，但本質卻是不變的，即不斷地渴望（ceaseless aspiring）卻又永遠地滿足（ceaseless content）。詩人渴望自己的心可以像噴水池一樣永保清新卻又不斷變化。

 詞藻釋義

☆ **nature**　*n.*　自然，本性，天性
　the nature of things 萬物的本質

☆ **tame**　*v.*　馴服
　He needs to tame his temper.
　他需要克制自己的脾氣。

重點句型

be 動詞＋形容詞＋*of*

詩中反覆用到 full of 這個形容詞片語，雖然之前介紹過 be full of 和 be filled with，但這裡要補充一些類似的形容詞片語，也就是 be 動詞＋形容詞＋of。

例如：be glad of、be scared of、be certain of、be fond of、be aware of、be capable of、be conscious of、be proud of、be afraid of、be jealous of、be tired of、be ashamed of 等。

這些片語後面都要接名詞或動名詞，是日常生活經常會用到的詞彙，務必要搞清楚並背得滾瓜爛熟。

寫作指引

噴泉給人一種不斷流動變化的感覺，其實本質就是一個水柱。也可把愛情視為一種多變卻又不變的關係。

愛情關係維持不變固然好，但如果流於形式或一成不變，就會產生危機。此時男女雙方就要試著做一些改變，讓愛情關係持續新鮮有趣。

範例

1
Part

2
Part

3
Part

There is no easy way to maintain a love relationship. As time passes, a relationship could fall into routine.

A relationship should be a safe haven for a man and the woman he loves. If the two are stuck in a rut, the safe haven is at the risk of collapsing.

I talk about this because I feel that we now have a similar problem. We need to work together to prevent the relationship from becoming too monotonous or too mundane. We can't just spend time together at a coffee shop.

We need to change.

With love.

中譯

維持愛情關係並不容易。時間一久，愛情關係可能流於形式。

愛情關係應該是戀愛中男女的避風港，如果兩人的關係變得一成不變，避風港就有坍塌的危機。

我這麼說是因為我感覺我們現在有類似的問題。我們必須一起努力不讓彼此的關係變得太過單調或平凡，不能只把時間消磨在咖啡館裡。

我們必須改變。

愛。

知識補給

　　美國 19 世紀文學家詹姆士・羅素・羅威爾（1819-1891）是美國浪漫派詩人，在世時是個重要的文壇人士，可是他的重要性到了 20 世紀卻逐漸下降。他出身於新英格蘭一個顯赫家族，並從哈佛大學取得法學學位，但和很多攻讀法律的文學家一樣，他也不務正業，反而對文學創作很有興趣。他的成名和一群稱為爐邊詩人（fireside poets）的新英格蘭詩人有關，這些詩人包括著名的亨利・沃茲沃思・朗費羅、威廉・卡倫・布萊恩特及羅威爾本人，他們是美國第一批可以和英國詩人相提並論的詩人，重要性不言可喻。羅威爾相信詩人可扮演先知和社會評論家的角色，進而推動社會改革，像是廢除黑奴運動。

Unit 10
think / consider
羅伯特·佛洛斯特《雪夜林邊駐足》
Robert Frost "Stopping by Woods on a Snowy Evening"

 Classic 經典詩句

My little horse must think it queer
To stop without a farmhouse near
Between the woods and frozen lake
The darkest evening of the year.

...

The woods are lovely, dark and deep,
But I have promises to keep,
And miles to go before I sleep,
And miles to go before I sleep.

　　四度獲得普立茲獎的美國大詩人羅伯特·佛洛斯特（Robert Frost）於 1922 年寫下這首大家耳熟能詳的《雪夜林邊駐足》，由於文字淺顯易懂，意象生動鮮明，讀者幾乎可以把整首詩背下，著名的詩句有：The woods are lovely, dark and deep, / But I have promises to keep, / And miles to go before I sleep, / And miles to go before I sleep（樹林美麗黑暗又深沈／然我有承諾在身／要走很長的路才能睡／要走很長的路才能睡）。本章節則要討論以下詩句內含的文法：My little horse must think it queer / To stop without a farmhouse near / Between the woods and frozen lake / The darkest evening of the year.（我的小馬肯定感到奇怪／歇在四處不見農家／寒林冰湖之間／一年最暗的黃昏）。

　　這首詩的敘述者在一個最黑的夜晚騎馬經過一處積滿了雪的樹林，他不知不覺愛上周遭的景致，因而暫停下來，他的馬覺得奇怪怎麼停在一個沒有人住的地方，因而拉了拉韁繩，敘述者想起他還有承諾的事項要做，要走很長的路才能躺下來休息。

詞藻釋義

☆ **dark** *adj.* 黑暗的

黑頭髮是 dark hair，比較少說 black hair。

☆ **promise** *n.* 諾言，約定

make a promise 是許下承諾之意。

think / consider

　　詩中用到 think it queer 這個句型，think 和 consider 之類的動詞經常後面接 it 作為虛受詞，帶出後面的不定詞（to+原形動詞）或 that 子句，這種句型很常用到。

　　例句：我們認為愛我們的父母很重要。
We think / consider it important to love our parents.
We think / consider it important that we love our parents.
這兩個句子意思一樣，可相互替換使用。

寫作指引

　　愛是一種責任，只要愛上了，就要愛到底，就像是要等到抵達目的地才能休息的旅人一般。

　　追求女人時要表現出責任感，除了表達愛意外，還要實現自己的承諾，這樣才能讓女人放心地跟著你，也就是說，愛是一種責任。

範例

Love is a responsibility. A man has to take care of the woman he loves, and it is the same the other way around. A woman wants not only love but also commitment from her lover. I can give you both.

I will love you for the rest of my life. Don't refuse to accept love just because men are vulnerable to the temptations of other women. I might be no exception, but I'll fulfill my commitment to you, which is to love you forever. That makes all the difference.

You need to be loved, and I am a man who you trust.

With love.

中譯

　　愛是一種責任。男人該照顧他愛的女人，反之亦然。女人不但需要愛人的愛，還需要他的承諾，我兩樣都能給妳。

　　我在接下來的生命中都會愛妳。不要因為男人無法抵抗其他女人的誘惑而拒絕接受愛情，我或許也不例外，但我會實現對妳的承諾，也就是永遠地愛妳。這是差別所在。

　　妳需要被愛，我則是一個妳可以信任的男人。

　　愛。

 知識補給

　　羅伯特‧佛洛斯特（1874-1963）在美國文學史上的地位不亞於前面介紹過的華特‧惠特曼和艾米莉‧狄更生，但他是比較近代的作家，算是有從前人的作品得到啟發的那一類。佛洛斯特於 1922 年寫下《雪夜林邊駐足》，兩年後第一次贏得普立茲獎，而他一生總共贏得四次普立茲獎。佛洛斯特的詩作以文字簡明扼要著稱，同時擅長描寫一般人的心境，他在這首短詩中運用戲劇獨白（dramatic monologue）方式呈現出一個暗夜獨自經過積雪樹林的旅者的心境，主人翁只是一般人，不是什麼特殊人物，這或許是他的詩所以能感動這麼多人的原因。他的詩雖然簡單，但在詮釋時還是有難度，像是詩中的 sleep 到底是指真的入睡還是暗指死亡，就引起不少的爭論。

Unit 11

be aware of
艾略特《歇斯底里》
T.S. Eliot "Hysteria"

Classic 經典詩句

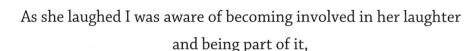

As she laughed I was aware of becoming involved in her laughter
and being part of it,
until her teeth were only accidental stars with a talent for squad-
drill.
I was drawn in by short gasps, inhaled at each momentary recovery,
lost finally in the dark caverns of her throat

　　在美國出生卻在 39 歲歸化為英國籍的艾略特（T.S. Eliot）是 20
世紀主要詩人之一，這首《歇斯底里》算是他的小品，描述的是一名女
人歇斯底里般的笑聲，著名的詩句為：As she laughed I was
aware of becoming involved in her laughter and being part of
it, until her teeth were only accidental stars with a talent for
squad-drill. I was drawn in by short gasps, inhaled at each
momentary recovery, lost finally in the dark caverns of her

throat（當她笑時，我意識到自己被捲入她的笑聲中，並成為其中一部分，直到她露出的牙齒成了零落的星點，閃爍著編貝的天資。我被短促的喘氣聲所吸引，每一短暫的恢復後又被吸入，最後迷失在她黑洞般的喉嚨之中）。

　　這首詩很有趣味，描寫的主題居然是一位女子歇斯底里般的笑聲。詩中的敘述者一方面被她的笑聲吸引，一方面又覺得反感想要加以抗拒，可是不知不覺之中卻像是被吸入黑洞一樣被她吞進喉嚨。她一開始笑，敘述者就覺得陷入她的笑聲之中。

☆ **gasp**　*n.*　喘氣

at the last gasp 是奄奄一息的意思。

☆ **inhale**　*v.*　吸氣，吸入

inhale deeply 是深深吸一口氣的意思。

☆ **cavern**　*n.*　洞穴，山洞

指的是大山洞，拿來比喻女子的喉嚨有點誇張。

重點句型

be aware of

詩中用到常見的片語 be aware of，意思是知道或意識到，相當於 be conscious of，be aware of the problem 是意識到問題，be aware of someone's absence 是意識到某人不在場，be aware of time 則是知道時間。

要注意 aware 有一類似的字詞，即 beware。

當我們說 Beware of the dog. 意思是當心那條狗，牠可能咬你。

Be aware of the dog. 則是要你小心不要踩到那隻狗，意思大不相同。beware 是動詞，後面接 of 表示當心和提防的意思。

寫作指引

女人有時候很情緒化，碰上這種狀況時可用幽默的方式化解自己感受到的震撼。

喜歡某一女人通常是因為她的外貌或談吐，也有人比較特別，會因為該名女子的笑聲而喜歡上她，只要結果一樣，過程如何並不重要。

範例

It is interesting to see you laugh. When you laugh a hearty laugh, I am deeply impressed by the way you let go your feeling.

You love to be free. I am a cautious and self-restrained man who doesn't know to express his feeling. You have something that I don't have. That's why I am attracted by you.

You might be surprised that a man likes you because of your laugh. Of course, you are attractive in many other aspects. It is just your laugh that touches me the most. It is true.

With love.

1
Part

2
Part

3
Part

中譯

　　看妳笑很有趣。當妳開懷大笑時，我對妳釋放情感的方式產生很深的印象。

　　妳愛好自由，我則過度小心和自我克制，不知如何表達自己的感情。妳具有我沒有的東西，這是我被妳吸引的原因。

　　妳或許對有人因妳的笑而喜歡妳感到驚訝，當然妳在其他方面也很吸引力，只是妳的笑最能打動我，真的。

　　愛。

知識補給

　　諾貝爾文學獎得主艾略特（1888-1965）最著名的作品之一是詩作《荒原》（The Waste Land），那是研究英國文學者的必讀作品。艾略特和文學創作的現代主義運動有很大的關係，他 1917 年創作的詩作《普魯弗洛克的情歌》（The Love Song of J. Alfred Prufrock）被認為是現代主義的起源。現代主義的特色是打破舊有的規則和傳統，不斷在形式和風格上進行實驗，以找出獨特的當代表達方式。《歇斯底里》這首短詩看起完全不像是傳統的詩，反而比較像是一篇短的散文，其實那就是艾略特刻意營造出來的一種散文詩，也就是自由詩，現代主義作品多的是這類嘗試，當然這些作品也在意象的表現上有所創新，像是這首短詩所用到的黑洞喉嚨比喻及新興的心理學分析技巧。

Unit 12

doubt
羅伯特・佛洛斯特《沒有走過的路》
Robert Frost "The Road Not Taken"

Classic 經典詩句

Yet knowing how way leads on to way,

I doubted if I should ever come back.

...

I shall be telling this with a sigh

Somewhere ages and ages hence:

Two roads diverged in a yellow wood, and I—

I took the one less traveled by,

And that has made all the difference.

　　羅伯特・佛洛斯特於 1916 年寫下這首知名度及閱讀率或許超過《雪夜林邊駐足》的《沒有走過的路》，著名的詩句為：I shall be telling this with a sigh / Somewhere ages and ages hence: / Two roads diverged in a yellow wood, and I— / I took the one less traveled by, / And that has made all the difference.（我以

後將用嘆息的口吻敘說這段／大概是多年多年以後／黃樹林中，分出兩條路，而我／我選擇了比較少人走過的路／那造就所有的不同）。本章節則要討論以下詩句內含的文法：Yet knowing how may leads on to way, / I doubted if I should ever come back.（我深知阡陌連遠途／我懷疑日後能否再回來）。

説文解詩

　　這首詩敘述在行走途中走到叉路口，敘述者猶豫了一下，不太確定要往哪條路走。他比較了一下，兩條路看起來差不多，但其中一條長了很多草，似乎比較需要人去磨一下（Because it was grassy and wanted wear），於是他就選擇這條比較少人走過的路。

詞藻釋義

☆ hence　*adv.*　今後
　　就是 from now 的意思，多在文學作品中出現，一般文章很少用。

☆ diverge　*v.*　分歧，分出
　　指路徑（path）或目標（objective）出現分歧。

doubt

詩中用到 doubt if 這個句型，意思是不確定所說的事是否為真或是否真的會發生，doubt 後面也可接 whether，意思相同，但如果後面接 that 子句，意思則不大相同。

例句：

I doubt whether he will help.

I doubt that he will help me.

前面的句子是我不確定他是是否會幫我，後面的句子是我懷疑他會幫我，兩個句子的意思全然不同，使用時要注意。

選愛人也像選路一樣，是選漂亮人人都想要的那一種，還是有內涵的那一種，都要做一番考量。

美麗的女人比比皆是，有內涵的女人卻越來越難找，但想要追有內涵的女人，也要自己有內涵才行，所謂話不投機半句多。

範例

It is easy to find a beautiful woman but it is hard to win her heart.

It is difficult to find a woman of substance, but it is easy to win her heart as long as you are a cultured man and have a good taste.

You are a woman of substance in my eyes. It does not mean that you are not physically attractive. It means that you have more to you than meets the eye.

I can see your beautiful mind. Beauty is only skin deep. You possess something deeper and nicer.

With love.

中譯

　　很容易找到美麗的女人，贏得她的心卻很難。

　　很難找有內涵的女人，贏得她的心卻很容易，只要你是個有教養和有品味的男人。

　　在我看來，妳就是個有內涵的女人，這不是在說妳外表不吸引人，而是妳擁有比外表看到還多的內涵。

　　我看得到妳美麗的心，美麗只有皮膚那一層深度，妳擁有更深沉和更好的東西。

　　愛。

知識補給

　　佛洛斯特根據自己的經驗創作出《雪夜林邊駐足》。他在 1912 至 1915 年間旅居英國，期間和英國作家愛德華・湯瑪士（Edward Thomas）成為好友。他們常常一起散步，湯瑪士多次在行走過程表現出無法決定走哪一條路的猶豫不決心態，這給佛洛斯特留下深刻的印象，他回到美國後根據此一經驗寫下這首廣受歡迎的詩。不過佛洛斯特原本只是想用這首詩來文雅地嘲弄一笑他的英國好友，沒想到一般讀者看了之後都認真地推敲詩中所蘊含的人生哲理，連湯瑪士本人也很認真，他後來決定投筆從戎上戰場（當時正值第一次世界大戰），結果不幸戰死。這個不幸的結局絕對不是佛洛斯特事先所能預想得到，只能說造化弄人。

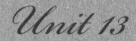

Unit 13

in fear of / for fear that
溫德爾·貝里《荒野景物間的平靜》
Wendell Berry "The Peace of Wild Things"

Classic 經典詩句

When despair for the world grows in me

and I wake in the night at the least sound

in fear of what my life and my children's lives maybe.

...

I come into the presence of still water.

And I feel above me the day-blind stars

waiting with their light. For a time

I rest in the grace of the world, and am free.

　　當代美國文學家溫德爾·貝里（Wendell Berry）在《荒野景物間的平靜》中表達人可在荒野或大自然中找到心靈的平靜，著名的詩句為：I come into the presence of still water. / And I feel above me the day-blind stars / waiting with their light. For a time / I rest in the grace of the world, and am free.（我進入靜水的領域

／且我感受到天上被白日遮住的星星／它們等著綻放出光芒。有一會兒／我歇息在世界的優雅之中，自由自在）。本章節則要討論以下詩句內含的文法：When despair for the world grows in me / and I wake in the night at the least sound / in fear of what my life and my children's lives maybe.（當我深感絕望之際／我在夜裡因為一丁點聲響醒來／恐懼我和孩子未來將會怎樣）。

說文解詩

當詩人感到絕望時，一丁點聲音都會讓他從睡夢中驚醒，擔心自己和他的小孩會發生什麼事，此時走到戶外的水域邊躺下，融入到荒野事物間的平靜，這些景物不會為生命預設悲傷。如此與大自然合而為一，詩人感覺受到恩寵，自由自在。

詞藻釋義

☆ **presence** *n.* 臨在，面前，存在

He honors us with his presence.

他的來到使我們感到榮耀。

☆ **still** *adv.* 還，仍，尚

He is still working hard.

他仍然辛苦地工作。

in fear of / for fear that

詩中用了 in fear of 這個片語，但現在比較少用，取而代之的是 for fear of 或 for fear that，都在表達擔心或唯恐之意。

例句：他提早半小時離開，以免錯過公車。
He left half an hour early for fear of missing the bus.
相當於 He left half an hour early for fear that he might miss the bus.

要注意，由於只是擔心事情的可能發生，所以要用表示推測的助動詞 might，如果沒有把握，就一直用 for fear of 就好，但記得 of 後面要接動名詞。for fear that 的 that 子句也不一定要用 might，也有用到其他助動詞，所以確實比較複雜一點。

在相對立的事物之間找到平衡和寧靜，有助於紓解自己的壓力，回復正常的生活。

要增進愛情關係，除了甜言蜜語和經常的關心外，還可一起參與活動，像是旅遊或野營，當然也要為這些活動賦予一些詩情畫意的想像空間。

範例

1
Part

2
Part

3
Part

I would like to invite you to go camping with me in the wilderness. I love nature especially as I feel down in spirits. I love plants, trees, flowers, and the beautiful starry night sky. I love sitting under a tree, either meditating or thinking nothing at all.

I used to do all these by myself. If you could go with me, it would mean a lot to me. You change my life. Solo travel is a wonderful experience, but it would be better with company. Such travel could be a life-changing experience for both of us.

With love.

中譯

　　我想要邀請妳和我一起到野外露營。我喜愛大自然，特別是情緒低落時。我喜歡草木、花朵和美麗的星空。我喜歡坐在樹下，可以做冥想或什麼也不想。

　　我以前都獨自做這些事情。如果妳能和我一起去，會對我產生很大的意義。妳改變了我的生命。獨自旅行是一種很棒的經驗，但如果有伴會更好。這種旅行會成為改變我們兩人生命的經歷。

　　愛。

知識補給

　　溫德爾‧貝里（1934-迄今）是當代美國文學家，以創作詩起家，也寫小説，近年更成為一名環境保育者，倡導人類應與大自然和諧相處的理念，自己也身體力行，在肯塔基州家鄉經營農場達 40 餘年。為了專心經營農場，他還辭去大學的教職，展現出他的言行一致。他在詩作中讚頌生命的神聖及日常生活中經常被視為理所當然的神奇之處，就像《荒野景物間的平靜》中所呈現的，詩人在情緒低到谷底之際，竟在平常熟悉的水域邊找到心靈的平靜，這種平靜存在於荒野的萬物之間，平靜與荒野這兩個看似對立的概念通常不會讓人聯想在一起，要經由心靈的沈澱，如同進入靜水的領域，才能體會大自然給予的恩寵，達到自由自在之境。

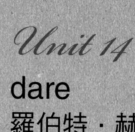

Unit 14
dare
羅伯特·赫立克《致伊萊翠》
Robert Herrick "To Electra"

Classic 經典詩句

I dare not ask to kiss,

I dare not beg a smile,

Lest having that, or this,

I might grow proud the while.

17 世紀英國詩人羅伯特·赫立克（Robert Herrick）以抒情詩著稱，在《致伊萊翠》中表達出一種有所節制的愛，著名的詩句為：I dare not ask to kiss, / I dare not beg a smile, / Lest having that, or this, / I might grow proud the while.（我不敢要求吻妳／我不敢乞求妳對我笑／以免得到妳的吻或妳的笑後／我會變得驕傲起來）。

 說文解詩

　　詩中敘述者說不敢向愛人要求親吻，也不敢要她給個笑容，因為他知道自己得到後就會驕傲起來，他只在心中渴望親到剛剛親吻到她的空氣，有點像是柏拉圖式愛情，卻也點出男人在得到女人的心或身體後，會變得驕傲，不再那麼珍惜所得到的一切。

 詞藻釋義

☆ **dare** *aux.* 敢，竟敢

　　作為助動詞用，和第三人稱單數主詞一起用時仍是原形，如 He dare not go out alone.

☆ **lest** *conj.* 唯恐，免得

　　17 世紀時的用法已相當於現在的用法。

重點句型

dare

詩中用到 dare 這個助動詞，dare 除了是助動詞外，也可作為一般動詞用，但兩種用法很不相同，使用時要注意。

作為助動詞時，dare 不管第幾人稱的單複數都是維持原形，如：He dare not fight. How dare you / he say such a thing?

否定時在後面加個 not 即可，過去式加 d 為 dared；作為一般動詞時，He dare not fight. 就成為 He does not dare to fight. 此時 dare 後面要加不定詞，這是它的動詞用法。

need 也是同時具有助動詞和一般動詞功能的字彙。

寫作指引

男人在得到女人的心或肉體後通常會變成另一個人，有此自覺並勇於承認的男人不多。

女人必須了解男人的天性，才能在戀愛時有所為有所不為，但不要把所有男人都一概而論，因為不是所有男人都以性愛為最終目的。

範例

I recently found a quote on the Internet– "What every man wants is a lady by day and a sexual goddess by night."

How true! As a woman, you should know something about it.

I am not saying this to imply that we should make love. I just want you to know the real nature of man. Nature is one thing, while nurture is quite another.

As a man is thinking about sex, he will not necessarily take action. Don't be intimidated by what other women say about men. Use your own judgment to find out what kind of man I am.

With love.

1
Part

2
Part

3
Part

中譯

　　我最近在網路上看到一句話：「每個男人想要的女人在白天是個淑女，夜晚時卻變成性感女神」。

　　說得多麼貼切！身為一個女人，妳應該知道一些。

　　我這麼說的目的不是在暗示我們應該做愛，我只是想讓妳了解男人的天性。天性是一回事，後天教養則是另一回事。

　　當男人想到性時，他不見得一定會採取行動。不要因其他女人對男人的說法而感到害怕，用妳自己的判斷力來看我是怎樣的男人。

　　愛。

知識補給

羅伯特·赫立克（1591-1674）一生寫了 2500 多首詩，大部分收錄在詩集《金蘋果園》（Hesperides）中，他最有名的詩作是《致少女們，珍惜時光》（To the Virgins, to Make Much of Time），這是一首提倡及時行樂（carpe diem）的詩，開頭第一句是：趁你還能的時候採摘玫瑰花蕾（Gather ye rose-buds while ye may）；接著又說：今天還在綻放微笑的同一朵花／明日將會凋謝消逝（And this same flower that smiles to-day, / To-morrow will be dying）。提起這首詩的原因是為了和《致伊萊翠》做一比較，為何同一詩人會寫出如此不同風格的詩作？赫立克擔任過神職人員，《致伊萊翠》的風格比較符合他的出世身份，但他卻在其他詩中讚美做愛和女性身體，這在當時確實有點前衛。

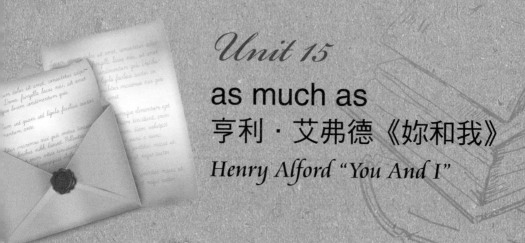

Unit 15
as much as
亨利·艾弗德《妳和我》
Henry Alford "You And I"

Classic 經典詩句

My hand is lonely for your clasping, dear;

My ear is tired waiting for your call.

I want your strength to help, your laugh to cheer;

Heart, soul and senses need you, one and all.

...

As much as love asks love, does thought ask thought.

Life is so short, so fast the lone hours fly,

We ought to be together, you and I.

19 世紀英國詩人亨利·艾弗德（Henry Alford）同時也具有神職人員身份，還是一名學者，《妳和我》這首詩表現出一種帶著靈性渴望的愛，其中著名的詩句為：My hand is lonely for your clasping, dear; / My ear is tired waiting for your call. / I want your strength to help, your laugh to cheer; / Heart, soul and senses

need you, one and all.（我寂寞的手渴望妳來緊握，親愛的／我疲憊的耳朵等著妳的呼喚／我需要妳的力量來協助我，妳的笑容來振奮我／我的心、靈魂和感官都需要妳，全都需要）。本章節則要討論以下詩句內含的文法：As much as love asks love, does thought ask thought. / Life is so short, so fast the lone hours fly, / We ought to be together, you and I.（愛要求相等的愛／關懷要求對等的關懷／人生苦短，歲月如流／我們應該在一起，妳和我）。

 說文解詩

　　這首詩的敘述者渴望得到愛人的緊握和呼喚，希望得到她的力量的支撐，她的笑容可以讓他開心，他的心、靈魂和感官都需要她。他因此敦促她和他在一起，因為雙方都有相同的渴望，且生命短暫，時光稍縱即逝。

 詞藻釋義

☆ clasp　*v.*　緊握，緊抱
要記得緊握某人的手是 clasp someone by the hand。

☆ sense　*n.*　感官
the (five) senses 就是五種感官，聽覺是 the sense of hearing，其他依此類推。

重點句型

as much as

詩中用到 as much as 這個慣用語，意思是多達，看起來很簡單，卻很容易出錯。

表示數量時，後面可接單數或複數名詞，此時複數名詞被視為單一數量，算是不可數，例如：It cost me as much as 500 dollars. He walks as much as ten kilometers each day.

表示程度時，as much as 後面可接 possible 或 one can，如：You need to rest as much as possible.（你需要盡量多休息。）I want to help you as much as I can.（我想要盡力幫你。）

另外 as much as 也可表示經常性，如：He does not go out as much as he used to.

寫作指引

西方人表達愛情比較直接，說愛就愛，除了心靈上的契合外，也要身體上的結合。

人的心會寂寞，手和耳朵也會寂寞，同樣也需要愛人的愛撫和呼喚，表達愛意要直接，不要拖拖拉拉浪費浪漫時刻。

範例

My hand longs for your clasping as much as my ear waits for your call. You give me strength and make me smile. My heart and soul need you. So does my body. We should be together. We want each other so much.

I always dream of you. I don't want you to live in my dream only. I want you to be part of my life. Life is short. There is no need to waste time on trifling things. We just need to make sure of one thing– you love me, and I love you, too.

With love.

1
Part

2
Part

3
Part

中譯

　　我的手渴望妳來緊握，而我的耳朵也同樣熱切地等待妳的呼喚。妳給了我力氣，讓我有了笑容。我的心和靈魂都需要妳。我們應該在一起，我們如此渴望對方。

　　我經常夢到妳，我不想讓妳只活在我的夢裡，我要妳成為我的生命的一部份。生命是短暫的，沒必要浪費時間在一些瑣事上，我們只要確定一件事就好—那就是妳愛我，而我也愛妳。

　　愛。

知識補給

英國詩人亨利·艾弗德（1810-1871）雖然不是英國文學史上的重要人物，但從這首《妳和我》可看出，他所呈現的是另一種趣味和意境，儘管不被當代或後世文壇奉為經典作家，但到了我們現在這個多元文化和價值的年代，或許可以重新審視他的作品價值及意義。出生於倫敦的艾弗德，家族五代都有人從事英國聖公會神職人員職務，他從小就顯露詩才，10 歲以前就寫出幾首拉丁文頌詩，稍大進入劍橋大學三一學院就讀。艾弗德對文壇的最大貢獻之一是他花了 20 年時間編輯出的《新約聖經》，他在裡面加入個人的註解和研究結果，有助於讀者更加了解《新約聖經》。

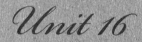

Unit 16

gaze、stare、gape、glare
海涅《當我注視妳的眼睛》

Heinrich Heine "When I Gaze into Your Eyes"

 Classic 經典詩句

When I gaze into your eyes,
All my pain and woe vanishes

　　19 世紀德國詩人海涅（Heinrich Heine）雖然以德文創作，但由於長年流亡在外國不見容於祖國，加上很多作品被翻譯成英文，所以英語系國家讀者反而很熟悉他的作品。《當我注視妳的眼睛》中的著名詩句為：When I gaze into your eyes, / All my pain and woe vanishes（當我注視妳的眼睛／我所有的痛苦和悲哀都消失）。

　　這首詩的敘述者說，當我注視妳的眼睛，我所有的痛苦和悲哀都消失；當我依靠著妳的胸部時，我有進入天堂的感覺，但當妳說「我愛你」時，我卻悲傷地哭了起來。這雖然不是愛到死去活來，卻也愛到哭到斷腸。

☆ **gaze**　*v.*　注視，凝視
gaze at the stars
凝視著星星

☆ **woe**　*n.*　悲哀，悲痛
主要用在詩歌中的驚嘆句。
Woe is me!
我真可悲！

重點句型

gaze、stare、gape、glare

詩中用 gaze 這個動詞來表達凝視和注視之意，類似的詞語有 look、stare、gape、glare 等。

look 泛指一般的看；gaze 是專注持續地看，表現驚奇和有興趣之意，如：gaze at the stars。

stare 是張大眼睛看著，原因是驚訝、好奇或心不在焉，如：It is impolite to stare at people.（盯著人看很不禮貌。）

gape 是天真無知地張大嘴巴看著，如：The child gaped at the elephant.（小孩目瞪口呆地看著大象。）

glare 是嚴厲或生氣地瞪著，如：He glared angrily at me.（他生氣地瞪著我。）另外，gaze 後面通常接 at，也可接 into。

寫作指引

愛情除了讓人愉快外，也具有療癒效果，可以讓心裡和肉體的痛苦減少。以實際例子說明愛的治療力量，只要看到愛人就不會感到痛苦，如果能親到她效果會更好，但這只是希望，目前還沒到這個程度。

範例

Love has healing power. Love gives us the strength to overcome problems. Love is within each and every one of us. Don't shut the door against love.

You don't know how much influence you could have on others. When I look into your eyes, all my pain seems to disappear. Love is such a wonderful thing. If I could kiss your lips, I would feel like in heaven.

All these are the therapeutic effects of love. I am not a patient asking for a prescription. I am just a poor man suffering from deficiency of love. I aspire for love from you.

With love.

中譯

　　愛有治療的力量。愛給我們克服困難的力量，愛存在於我們每一人的內心，不要關上門拒絕愛。

　　妳不知道妳對其他人有多大的影響。當我注視妳的眼睛時，我所有的痛苦似乎都消失，愛是如此地奇妙。如果我能親吻妳的嘴唇，我會感覺像是到了天堂。

　　凡此種種都是愛的療效。我不是尋求醫療處方的病人，而是因缺乏愛而受苦的可憐男人。我渴望得到妳的愛。

　　愛。

知識補給

　　海涅（1797-1856）是 19 世紀德國最重要的詩人之一，屬於浪漫派詩人，從《當我注視妳的眼睛》便可看出他的浪漫情懷。在德國作家當中，他是作品被翻譯為外國語言最多的一個。不過他的個性及言論似乎不見容於當時的祖國普魯士，因為他喜歡評論和議論，對國家的書報審查制度很有意見，1831 年後他離開德國到巴黎展開流亡生活，1833 年他的作品在普魯士遭禁，原因是不讓普魯士的道德和紀律受到破壞。他雖然在巴黎過著流亡的生活，但也吸取大量的不同思潮及作品，進而寫下大量的作品，算是有得也有失。詩人的浪漫和自由之心總是不見容於僵化的政治教條和傳統文化。

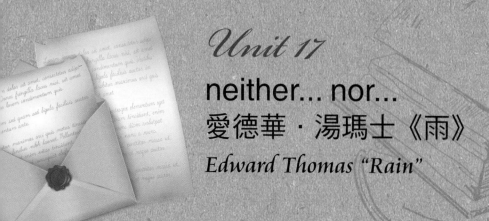

Unit 17
neither... nor...
愛德華‧湯瑪士《雨》
Edward Thomas "Rain"

 **Classic** 經典詩句

Rain, midnight rain, nothing but the wild rain

On this bleak hut, and solitude, and me

Remembering again that I shall die

And neither hear the rain nor give it thanks

For washing me cleaner than I have been

死於第一次世界大戰的英國詩人愛德華‧湯瑪士（Edward Thomas）在這首《雨》中想像戰場上的死亡，著名的詩句為：Rain, midnight rain, nothing but the wild rain / On this bleak hut, and solitude, and me / Remembering again that I shall die / And neither hear the rain nor give it thanks / For washing me cleaner than I have been（雨，午夜的雨，只見狂暴的雨／降在這個荒涼的營舍上，降在孤獨上，降在我的身上／我想起我終要死去／聽不見雨聲也不感激它／儘管它把我洗得比原來還乾淨）。

 說文解詩

　　敘述者是一個戰場上的士兵，他在雨中想像可能發生的死亡，他不斷用「孤寂」和「孤單」這幾個字眼來強調自己身處戰場的無助。那是一種夾處在活人和死人之間的無助，他預見了死亡，水面漂浮的無數蘆葦象徵著眾多死亡士兵的屍體。

詞藻釋義

☆ **bleak** *adj.* 荒涼的，蕭瑟的
The economic outlook is bleak.
經濟前景黯淡。

☆ **solitude** *n.* 孤獨，孤寂
a life of solitude
孤獨的生活

重點句型

neither... nor...

詩中用到 neither... nor... 這個句型，看其用法似乎和現在並無不同。neither... nor... 是用來連接兩個否定的概念，可連接主詞、動詞、或主詞補語。

例句：

I neither smoke nor drink.（我不抽菸也不喝酒。）

He is neither friendly nor easy to get to along with.（他沒有很好相處。）

Neither John nor Mary wants to go.（約翰和瑪莉都不想去。）

要注意的是，neither... nor... 通常只連結兩個字詞，但有時也可連結兩種以上字詞，例如：He neither smiled, frowned, nor spoke.（他不笑不皺眉，也不說話。）另外，neither... nor... 連接兩個主詞時，後面的動詞要跟著第二個主詞變化，例如：Neither you nor anybody else is able to do this.（沒有人能夠做這個。）

寫作指引

面對未知的未來或確定發生的不幸，任何人都會有恐懼之心，能把這種恐懼書寫出來，也是一種解脫。

情侶在規劃未來時要面對現實，也就是在收入有限的狀況下，只能逐步往目標邁進，無法一蹴而成，必須先有這個共識才行。

範例

In the face of an uncertain future, we should be optimistic. I was not born rich. I am not earning much. Fortunately, I am not heavily in debt. I have to pay back some installment loans.

If you want me to buy a house for you, I can tell you that it is beyond my capability for the moment. But I can promise you a future. You have to help me first.

Your love can stimulate me to work harder. Let's build our future together. The best part of life is having a partner.

With love.

中譯

　　面對不確定的未來，我們應該保持樂觀。我不是生來就有錢，也賺得不多。不過幸好負債不多，只有一些分期貸款要償還。

　　如果妳要我為妳買棟房子，我可以告訴妳，我現在沒有這個能力。但我可以許妳一個未來。妳必須先幫我才行。

　　妳的愛將使我更努力工作，讓我們一起打造我們的未來。生命最好的一部份就是有個伴侶。

　　愛。

知識補給

　　被歸類為戰場詩人的愛德華・湯瑪士（1878-1917），其實本來並不一定要到位於法國的戰場前線，可是他志願要去，結果不幸被砲擊身亡，魂斷異鄉。之前介紹美國大詩人佛洛斯特所寫的《雪夜林邊駐足》時，曾提及佛洛斯特在英國期間常與湯瑪士一起在林間散步，湯瑪士在碰到交叉路口時總是顯得猶豫不決，佛洛斯特回美國後根據此一經驗寫下這首廣受歡迎的詩，似乎有點在開這位英國朋友的玩笑，誰知最後的結果是湯瑪士選擇走上一條似乎注定回不來的路，令人不勝唏噓。作為一名作家，湯瑪士的收入並不高，所以才會選擇從軍。在死亡前的 2 年從軍期間，他總共寫了 140 多首詩。

Part 3
沒有你的日子：思念

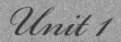

Unit 1
形容詞子句
康拉德・艾肯《我聽到的音樂》
Conrad Aiken "Music I Heard"

 **Classic 經典詩句**

Music I heard with you was more than music,
And bread I broke with you was more than bread.
Now that I am without you, all is desolate,
All that was once so beautiful is dead.

　　美國詩人康拉德·艾肯（Conrad Aiken）在《我聽到的音樂》這首詩中用簡明的文字營造出鮮明的意象，其中著名的詩句為：Music I heard with you was more than music, / And bread I broke with you was more than bread. / Now that I am without you, all is desolate, / All that was once so beautiful is dead.（和妳一起聽過的音樂已不只是音樂，／和妳一起分享的麵包也不只是麵包。／現在沒了妳，一切都變成如此淒涼，／原本美麗的一切都變得死氣沈沈。）

說文解詩

　　這首詩的作者為美國現代作家康拉德·艾肯（1889-1973），他的作品不僅有詩作，還包括小說、短篇小說及劇本。這首詩描述詩人（詩裡的敘述者，不等同於作者）對已不在身邊的她的思念，所謂睹物思人，她以前碰過的桌子、銀器、及玻璃杯，都勾起詩人的回憶。

詞藻釋義

☆ **desolate** *adj.* 荒蕪的，無人煙的；
孤寂的，淒涼的，被遺棄的
這個形容詞通常放在名詞之前描述某個地點、建築或人物的被遺棄、了無人煙、及孤寂狀態，很少直接作為主詞補語，就像這裡所見到的。

☆ **break** *v.* 打破，折斷，使碎裂
詩中指的是撕開麵包的動作。

重點句型

形容詞子句

　　這首詩中出現好幾個形容詞子句，如：（that 或 which）I heard with you 和(that 或 which) I broke with you，括號內是被省略的關係代名詞 that 或 which。

　　關係代名詞所引導的形容詞子句是在修飾前面的先行詞（人或物或事），關係代名詞分為主格（等於形容詞子句中的主詞），有 who（人）、which（物或事）、及 that（人或物或事情），受格關係代名詞則有 who（人）、whom（人）、which（物或事）、that（人或事或物），還有所有格關係代名詞 whose（人或人以外）。

　　Music (that or which) I heard with you 和 Bread (that or which) I broke with you 中的先行詞是 music 和 bread，關係代名詞 that 或 which 是功能為受格的關係代名詞，通常都可以省略，但主格和所有格關係代名詞則不可以省略，記住受格關係代名詞可有可無，不管是人或事或物，都可以用 that 作為關係代名詞。

寫作指引

　　形容詞子句是寫作時一定會用的句型，但通常會把 that 或 which 省略，以下範例有用到這類句子。依據這篇詩作，可寫出一篇以思念不在身邊的戀人為主題的情書。

範例

The days are hard for me as you are not with me. I miss every moment with you, either at a music concert or at the breakfast table.

I remember the soft touch of your hand and the passion in your eyes. I can feel your presence by looking at the tea cup you usually use.

Send messages to me as you are free. Just a few words from you would make me happy for a whole day. Keep me posted on how you are doing. Looking forward to your return.

With love.

中譯

　　妳不在我身邊的日子很難熬，我思念著與妳在一起的時光，不管是在聽音樂會時，還是在吃早餐時。

　　我記得妳溫柔的撫摸及眼中的熱情，只要看著妳以前常用的茶杯就能感覺到妳的存在。

　　有空傳訊息給我，簡短的幾句話就能讓我高興一整天。隨時讓我知道妳的最新動態。期待妳的歸來。

　　愛。

 知識補給

　　許多評論家把這篇詩作詮釋為年幼喪母的作者對母親的思念，此一以作者生平為主要詮釋依據的説法固然有其道理，但英文文學理論也有相當多學者主張，作者歸作者，作品歸作品，兩者不全然相等，也不可混為一談。以此詩為例，要解釋成作者對母親的思念也可以，但亦可適用於失去戀人的一般人，這種失去不見得是因為戀人死去，雖然詩中有某種程度的死亡寓意（connotation），但越是好的文學作品，詮釋的空間就越大，換句話説，就是想像的空間越大。也有可能是詩人（詩中的第一人稱敘述者）單方面緬懷一段逝去的戀情。

Unit 2
複合關係代名詞
比利・柯林斯《健忘》
Billy Collins "Forgetfulness"

Classic 經典詩句

The name of the author is the first to go

followed obediently by the title, the plot,

the heartbreaking conclusion, the entire novel

which suddenly becomes one you have never read,

never even heard of

...

Whatever it is you are struggling to remember,

it is not poised on the tip of your tongue

or even lurking in some obscure corner of your spleen

當代美國詩人比利・柯林斯（Billy Collins）在這首《健忘》中以輕鬆幽默的方式面對逐漸發生的健忘狀況，著名的詩句為：The name of the author is the first to go / followed obediently by the title, the plot, / the heartbreaking conclusion, the entire novel /

which suddenly becomes one you have never read, never even heard of（作者的名字首先從腦海消失／接下來是書名、情節／令人心碎的結局、整本小說／突然之間變成你從沒讀過，從未聽過的東西）。本章節則要討論以下詩句內含的文法：Whatever it is you are struggling to remember, / it is not poised on the tip of your tongue / or even lurking in some obscure corner of your spleen（無論你多麼努力要記住／它就是無法停留在你的舌尖上／或是潛伏在你脾臟中某個隱匿的角落）。

說文解詩

　　詩人以輕鬆幽默的方式面對逐漸惡化的健忘狀況，最先是忘記一本書的作者，接下來連書名和情節也忘了，連以前看了很感動的結局都不記得。其他的記憶也在消失，像是某一州的州花、某位親戚的住址、巴拉圭的首都等。之後再怎麼努力也無法記住。

詞藻釋義

☆ obediently　*adv.*　服從地，順從地
sit obediently in the chair 順從地坐在椅子上

☆ heart-breaking　*adj.*　令人傷心
the heart-breaking moment 令人心碎的一刻

重點句型

複合關係代名詞

　　詩中用到複合關係代名詞 whatever，這類的字詞還有 whoever、whichever，whenever 和 wherever 則是復合關係副詞。whatever 等複合關係代名詞包含了先行詞，所以不用再加關係代名詞，ever 是表示任何之意。

　　例句：

The club admits whoever pays the membership fee.

這裡的 whoever 就等於 anyone who。

You can take whatever you like.

這裡的 whatever 等於 anything that / which。

Help yourself to whichever you like.

這裡的 whichever 等於 anything that / which。

　　這些複合關係代名詞也可引導表示讓步的副詞子句，例如：

Whatever happens, I will always support you.

寫作指引

　　以正面的態度接受身體的退化，可開啟另一種可能性，即把過去大家避免談論的議題攤在陽光下。我們的寫作範例基本上都是以年輕人作為對象，但健忘這類議題不適合年輕人，所以這篇改以中年大叔為主角，他們還是有尋求愛情的機會和權利。

範例

As an older man seeking remarriage, I find it is not easy to remember all our dates as clearly as you. You have a good memory, while I begin to lose my memory, but only in bits and pieces. I can still remember most of the things.

I am now in my 50s. Strictly speaking, I am not an old man yet. I am just an older man looking for a wife. Every age has its charm and wisdom that really does come with age. You might not agree with me, since you are not my age yet.

With love.

1
Part

2
Part

3
Part

中譯

作為一個尋求再婚的年紀較大男子，我發現不太能像妳一樣把我們的約會都記得那麼清楚。妳的記憶力很好，而我則開始喪失記憶，但只有一點點，仍記得大部分事情。

我現在 50 多歲，嚴格說起來還不算是老人，只是一個在找老婆的年紀較大男子。每一個年紀都有其魅力，且智慧真的會隨年齡增長。妳或許不同意，因為妳還不到我的年紀。

愛。

知識補給

　　比利．柯林斯（1941-迄今）被譽為「美國最受歡迎的詩人」，他以幽默的口吻道出一些他對尋常事物的深刻觀察，像是在和讀者對話一般，因此很能打動讀者的心。柯林斯曾在 2001 至 2003 年間兩度擔任美國的桂冠詩人，2004 至 2006 年則是紐約州的桂冠詩人。他在 1990 年代末期的稿費就很驚人，可預支 6 位數的預付款，可謂名利雙收。2002 年，擔任美國桂冠詩人的柯林斯獲邀為 911 紐約市雙子星大樓恐怖攻擊事件撰寫一首紀念詩，並在紀念會的現場朗讀這首詩。看似風光的柯林斯，其實要到 1991 年，也就是 50 歲時，才真正得到美國文壇的重視，之前也經歷過很長的努力過程。柯林斯在寫作時心中總是有個讀者，他試著和這個讀者對話，從頭到尾。

Unit 3
動名詞的功能
哈里利・紀伯倫《論痛苦》
Khalil Gibran "On Pain"

Classic 經典詩句

Your pain is the breaking of the shell that encloses your
understanding.

Even as the stone of the fruit must break, that its heart may stand
in the sun, so must you know pain.

And you would accept the seasons of your heart,
even as you have always accepted the seasons that
pass over your fields.

And you would watch with serenity through the
winters of your grief.

　　黎巴嫩裔美國當代詩人哈里利・紀伯倫（Khalil Gibran）在《論痛苦》中說人的許多痛苦是自己所造成，但這些痛苦也是治療自己的藥方。著名的詩句為：And you would accept the seasons of your heart, / even as you have always accepted the seasons that /

pass over your fields. / And you would watch with serenity through the / winters of your grief.（且你將接受自己內心的四季／就如同接受降臨大地的／四季一般／且你將在如冬天的悲傷中／平靜地看著）。本章節則要討論以下詩句內含的文法：Your pain is the breaking of the shell that encloses your understanding. / Even as the stone of the fruit must break, that is heart may stand in the sun, so must you know pain.（你的痛苦是破繭而出的領悟／如同種籽得破殼而出，它的心靈才得以沐浴在陽光下）。

說文解詩

　　詩的第一句鏗鏘有力：你的痛苦打破阻礙你理解的外殼。因為有了痛苦，才能打開思想上的枷鎖，日常生活還是有許多的神奇事物。許多痛苦是自己所造成，但這種痛苦也是治療自己的藥方，雖然吃起來很苦，且用來吃藥的杯子還會燙口，但這個杯子可是被喻為製陶者的造物主用眼淚製成。

詞藻釋義

☆ **serenity**　*n.*　寧靜，沈著
　regain serenity
　重新恢復平靜

重點句型

動名詞的功能

在"Your pain is the breaking of the shell that encloses your understanding"這個詩句中，breaking 是一個動名詞，所謂動名詞就是由動詞變成的名詞，型態和現在分詞一模一樣，但現在分詞是作為補語或修飾名詞的形容詞，動名詞則是名詞功能。

例句：

Sleeping too much is not good for your health. 動名詞 sleeping 是句子的主詞。

I enjoy reading. 動名詞 reading 是動詞 enjoy 的受詞。

He gave up smoking. 動名詞 smoking 是動詞片語 give up 的受詞。

He left without saying goodbye. 動名詞 saying 是介系詞 without 的受詞。

寫作指引

把痛苦比喻為自我治療的藥方，算是一種妙喻，寫作有時把兩樣相反或不相干的概念或事物做一對比，會產生意想不到的特殊效果。

談情說愛到一個階段，就要開始規劃嚴肅的事情，像是互相給予承諾之類，一直拍拖下去也不是辦法。這樣才能永遠沐浴在春風之中。

範例

As the seasons of a year, there are also seasons in one's heart. Meeting you is in the spring. Hanging out with you is in the summer. Now we wait for the autumn to come, followed by the winter. What will happen next?

After all the happy moments that we have been together, we should prepare for something different. Should we go on like this or start thinking about our future? Are you expecting a commitment from me? If so, I can give you now. In doing so, we can skip the autumn and the winter and stay in the spring forever.

With love.

中譯

　　如同一年有四季般，人的心中也有四季。與妳相遇是在春天，與妳拍拖是在夏季。現在我們等待秋天的來臨，接著就是冬季。接下來會發生什麼？

　　在我們經歷過這麼多的快樂時光後，應該做點不同的準備。我們該這樣下去還是開始思考我們的未來？妳在期待我給妳承諾嗎？如果是，我現在就可以給妳。這樣一來，我們就可以跳過秋天和冬天，永遠待在春天。

　　愛。

知識補給

　　哈里利・紀伯倫（1883-1931）十幾歲就和家人從黎巴嫩移民到美國波士頓，學藝術的他以寫作為志業，不但以英文創作，也用阿拉伯文寫作。1923 年出版的《先知》（The Prophet）一書，奠定他在英語世界的地位。根據維基百科的説法，紀伯倫的作品銷售量在歷來所有詩人當中排名第三，僅次於英國的莎士比亞和中國的老子。紀伯倫擅長以散文詩（prose poetry)形式創作，作品中經常探討普世之愛（universal love)和精神上的愛（spiritual love），也就是與基督教有關的主題。在《論痛苦》一詩中，紀伯倫就用隱喻的方式多次提及造物主，如 the Unseen 和 the Potter。造物主引導我們用痛苦治療自己，並為我們製造用來吃藥的杯子，雖然喝藥時杯子會燙口，造物主在製造杯子時可是把自己的眼淚混入黏土之中成為製作的原料。

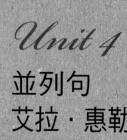

Unit 4
並列句
艾拉‧惠勒‧威爾考克斯《孤獨》
Ella Wheeler Wilcox "Solitude"

Classic 經典詩句

Sing, and the hills will answer;

Sigh, it is lost on the air;

The echoes bound to a joyful sound,

But shrink from voicing care.

　　美國女詩人艾拉‧惠勒‧威爾考克斯（Ella Wheeler Wilcox）最有名的作品之一就是這首《孤獨》，著名的詩句為：Sing, and the hills will answer; / Sigh, it is lost on the air; / The echoes bound to a joyful sound, / But shrink from voicing care.（唱個歌，山丘會回應／嘆口氣，則隨空氣消失／快樂的聲音產生回聲／擔憂的聲音減少回聲）。

說文解詩

　　這首詩雖然名為《孤獨》，但內容比較像是反孤獨，因為開頭就說「笑，世界跟著你笑」，可是哭只能獨自哭泣，言下之意就是要與人共享歡笑，這樣自己快樂別人也快樂，快樂的大殿容得下一列巨大氣派的火車，可是痛苦的通道卻很狹窄，還要排隊通過。

詞藻釋義

☆ **echo**　*n.*　回聲，共鳴
詩中指的是歌聲在山間產生的回聲。

☆ **bound**　*v.*　跳起，彈起
bound to one's feet
一躍而起

☆ **shrink**　*v.*　縮小，變小
shrink out of shape
衣服縮小得走樣

並列句

詩中反覆用到祈使句和 and / or 構成的並列句，像是"Laugh, and the world laughs with you" 和"Sing, and the hills will answer"，意思是如果怎樣就會怎樣，相當於 if 句型。

例句：如果你再做那件事一次，你將會有麻煩。

Do that again and you will be in trouble.等於 If you do that again, you will be in trouble.

如果用 or 來連接兩個子句，意思是如果不怎樣就會怎樣。

例句：閉嘴，不然你會有麻煩。

Shut up or you'll be in trouble.等於 If you don't shut up, you'll be in trouble.

作家是公眾人物，一言一行都會影響到讀者或追隨者，總是要提升大家的正向能量才行。

以戀愛產生正向能量為論點，試圖說服女方接受自己的邀請，被拒絕的感覺很不好，誰都不想遭到這樣的對待，這算是一種哀兵策略。

範例

When we fall in love, we create positive energy for each other. We make each other a better person. But the premise is that both sides like each other. If it is a one-sided crush, negative energy will take place.

Don't turn away from your admirers. Take them as your friends even if you don't want to develop a relationship with any of them. Being rejected is not a pleasant experience.

Positive energy is there for the taking. Why not accept my invitation and go out with me? It is good for both of us.

With love.

中譯

　　我們戀愛時為彼此帶來正向的能量，讓彼此變得更好，但前提是彼此喜歡。如果是單相思，負面能量就會取而代之。

　　不要不理妳的仰慕者，即使不想和他們發展愛情關係，也可以把他們當成朋友。被拒絕並不好受。

　　正向能量隨手可取。何不接受我的邀請和我一起出去？這對我們兩個都有好處。

　　愛。

 知識補給

　　《孤獨》是艾拉・惠勒・威爾考克斯（1850-1919）最有名的作品之一，其中最有名的詩句就是「笑，世界跟著你笑／哭，只能獨自哭泣」，筆者在前面的經典詩句選了其他詩句，因為好的詩句太多，不妨讓讀者欣賞一下其他以前比較少人注意到的詩句。根據威爾考克斯傳記中記載，威爾考克斯會寫下《孤獨》這首詩，是因為有次在火車上看到對面坐著一位暗自哭泣的黑衣婦人，這位婦人顯然剛失去心愛的丈夫，威爾考克斯有感而發，於是寫出這首傳頌至今的好詩，當年她投稿到報紙的稿費是 15 美元。她在作品中提倡正向思考（positive thinking）及自我依靠（self-reliant），希望人們藉此度過人生的逆境。

Unit 5
虛主詞 it
大衛・赫伯・勞倫斯《鋼琴》
D. H. Lawrence "Piano"

Classic 經典詩句

Softly, in the dusk, a woman is singing to me;

Taking me back down the vista of years, till I see

A child sitting under the piano, in the boom of the tingling strings

And pressing the small, poised feet of a mother who smiles

as she sings.

...

So now it is vain for the singer to burst into clamour

With the great black piano appassionato.

　　英國文學家大衛・赫伯・勞倫斯（D. H. Lawrence）在這首《鋼琴》中用鋼琴喚起兒時的記憶，著名的詩句為：Softly, in the dusk, a woman is singing to me; / Taking me back down the vista of years, till I see / A child sitting under the piano, in the boom of the tingling strings / And pressing the small, poised feet of a mother who smiles as she sings（輕輕地，一位婦女為我唱歌／把我引入過往的時光，直到我看到／一個坐在鋼琴底下、被叮噹琴弦聲環繞的小孩／他正用手觸碰邊唱歌邊面露微笑的母親懸空踩著踏板的小腳）。本章節則要討論以下詩句內含的文法：So now it is vain for the singer to burst into clamour / With the great black piano appassionato.（所以那歌者突然喧鬧／和著熱情洋溢的黑鋼琴，也是徒然）。

 說文解詩

詩人聽到一個女人唱歌時想到兒時看著母親彈鋼琴的情景，他當時坐在鋼琴下觸碰母親踩著踏板的腳。他想起過去星期天在家中舒服的客廳裡隨著鋼琴伴奏唱起讚美詩的時光，這與戶外的冬季景物形成對比。兒時回憶襲上心頭，詩人像個小孩一樣哭了起來。

 詞藻釋義

☆ vista　*n.*　遠景，回顧，展望
a postcard vista of rolling hills 如明信片般的起伏丘陵遠景

☆ boom　*n.*　隆隆聲，嗡嗡聲
the boom of tingling strings 隆隆的琴弦聲

重點句型

虛主詞 *it*

英文中經常見到 it 作為虛主詞的句型，尤其是碰到不定詞片語、動名詞和 that 子句時。例句：To have a driver's license is necessary. 以不定詞片語為主詞的頻率比不上加入 it 虛主詞的頻率——It is necessary to have a driver's license.（有駕照是必要的。）

Living in the mountains is enjoyable.（住山上很快樂。）可改為 It is enjoyable living in the mountains.

That you get up early is important.（早起很重要。）可改為 It is important that you get up early.

除了可作為 that 字句的虛主詞外，it 也可當成 whether 子句的虛主詞，如：It matters a lot whether she comes or not.（她是否要來很重要。）

寫作指引

回憶是每個人最大的寶庫，有著取之不盡用之不竭的資源，如能訴諸文字，當然更好。現在與過去及現實與記憶之間的關係，總能引發諸多的討論，不管怎樣，把握當下充實過活才是正道，就算成了回憶，也是快樂的回憶。

範例

1
Part

2
Part

3
Part

Memory is a treasure, while life is a blessing. A famous quote runs as follows: "You will never known the true value of a moment until it becomes a memory."

As time passes, our memories pile up. But as we get new memories, we lose some old ones.

I cherish every moment I spend with you. Such moment can never become a memory to me since I re-live it every day as I am with you. How wonderful it is! Seize the moment and live life to the fullest. That's the only thing I need to know.

With love.

中譯

　　記憶是一個寶庫，生命是一種恩賜。有句著名的話如下：「你永遠不知道某一時刻的真正價值，直到那一時刻成了回憶為止」。

　　隨著時間過去，我們的記憶逐漸累積。但是當我們有了新的回憶時，會失去某些舊的回憶。

　　我珍惜與妳在一起的每一刻，這些時刻不會成為我的回憶，因為我每天和妳在一起時都在重新過這些時刻。多棒啊！抓住當下那一刻，充實地過生活。我只要了解這些就好。

　　愛。

 知識補給

　　大衛‧赫伯‧勞倫斯（1885-1930）是 20 世紀主要的英國文學
作家之一，但在世時卻是個爭議性人物，因為他的作品中，主要是指小
說，牽涉到性愛及同性戀等當時社會仍無法接受公開討論的主題，但以
現在的觀點來看，勞倫斯的作品已經不算太驚世駭俗。同時代小說家福
斯特（E. M. Forster）在勞倫斯死後獨排眾議稱他為「我們這個世代
最具有想像力的小說家」，極具影響力的當代英國文學評論家李維斯
（F. R. Leavis）更將勞倫斯的小說列入他所稱英文小說的「偉大傳
統」，成為經典作品的一部分，也就是研讀英國文學者的必讀作品。勞
倫斯比較為人所知的是他的小說，像一度被列為禁書的《查泰萊夫人的
情人》，他的詩作反而比較少人知道。

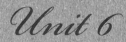

Unit 6
no time to+動詞
威廉・亨利・戴維斯《空閒》
William Henry Davies "Leisure"

What is this life if, full of care,

We have no time to stand and stare.

No time to stand beneath the boughs

And stare as long as sheep or cows.

　　英國威爾斯詩人威廉・亨利・戴維斯（William Henry Davies）在這首《空閒》中感嘆人們沒有花時間好好欣賞周邊的景物和眼前的人們，著名的詩句為：What is this life if, full of care, / We have no time to stand and stare. / No time to stand beneath the boughs / And stare as long as sheep or cows.（生命會是怎樣，如果充滿了憂慮／我們沒時間站著凝視／沒時間站在樹下／像羊或牛一樣長時間凝視）。

 說文解詩

　　現代生活由於工業化和都市化的影響，很少人會花時間仔細觀看周遭的景物或眼前的人們。為何不能像牛羊一樣站在樹下凝視？我們沒時間好好看看經過的樹林和其間的松鼠，也沒時間注意到，溪水在陽光照射下所呈現出的波光粼粼，其實和夜晚的閃爍星光並無二致。

 詞藻釋義

☆ **stare** *v.* 凝視，盯著看

stare at

盯著看

☆ **bough** *n.* 大樹枝

rest a fishing rod against a pine bough

把釣魚桿靠在松樹的樹枝上

no time to＋動詞

詩中反覆用到 no time to＋動詞這個句型，意思是沒有時間做什麼事情。to＋原形動詞是不定詞片語，這裡是用來修飾前面的名詞 time。前面的單元已介紹過不定詞片語，這裡就探討一些常見的 no time to 詞語，例如：no time to explain、no time to sleep、no time to spare、no time to waste 等。

當有人説"We have no room to spare"時，意思是我們沒有多餘的房間，也可説成"We have no spare room"，但不是每個跟在 no time to 後面的動詞都能如此替換。

寫作也是一種紓壓方式，可把內心的鬱悶發洩出來，但現代人忙於工作，只有在社群媒體上抒發一下自我。

除了寫作，戶外活動也是很好的舒壓方式，更是男女交往期間的必做事項，但如果女方不喜歡曬太陽，就得用文字説服她。

範例

Gone are those days when we could have time to sit under a tree and do nothing at all for a long stretch of time.

When was the last time we were lying on the grass gazing at stars? How long ago was it that we went to a concert or watch a drama performance in a theater? Not that I can remember.

Can we have more time to be together? Let's start with an outing to the seaside, where we can enjoy the sea breeze and get a good tan on the beach. Isn't it wonderful?

With love.

中譯

　　以前我們有空閒時間可以坐在樹下好一段時間什麼事也不做，那樣的日子早已不在。

　　我們上次躺在草地上觀賞星星是何時？我們多久以前去聽過音樂會或到劇場看戲劇表演？我不記得了。

　　我們能有多一點相處的時間嗎？先從海邊開始，那裡有海風，還可以做日光浴。這樣不是很棒嗎？

　　愛。

知識補給

　　出身自威爾斯的英國詩人威廉‧亨利‧戴維斯（1871-1940）一生困苦，曾當過流浪漢在街頭行乞。他沒受過太多的教育，卻能寫出這麼好的作品，實在令人敬佩。他的作品經常反映出生命中的困頓及人與大自然的關係。他在 22 歲靠著一小筆遺產就到美國展開長達 6 年的探險暨流浪生活，28 歲時因跳火車意外弄斷了一隻腳，之後回到英國才展開創作的生涯。他的創作之途也充滿艱辛，除了自費印刷外，還得挨家挨戶兜售他的作品，直到碰到賞識他的伯樂才出現轉機。從《空閒》這首詩可看出作者希望人們有多一點時間關注周遭的人和景物，我們可曾花時間好好看一個笑容是如何從眼睛開展到嘴巴（No time to wait till her mouth can / Enrich that smile her eyes began）。

Unit 7
it is evident that...
伊莉莎白・畢夏普《一種藝術》
Elizabeth Bishop "One Art"

Classic 經典詩句

The art of losing isn't hard to master;

so many things seem filled with the intent

to be lost that their loss is no disaster.

...

It's evident that art of losing's not too hard to master

though it may look like (Write it!) like disaster.

在美國女詩人伊莉莎白・畢夏普（Elizabeth Bishop）所寫的《一種藝術》中，所謂的藝術就是失去的藝術，頗有逆向思考式的味道，著名的詩句為：The art of losing isn't hard to master; / so many things seem filled with the intent / to be lost that their loss is no disaster.（失去這種藝術並不難掌握／許多事物似乎充滿了被失去的意向／失去了它們也就不構成災難）。本章節則要討論以下詩句內含的文法：It's evident that art of losing's not too hard to master / though it may look like (Write it!) like disaster.（這是失去的藝術並不難掌握的證據／雖然或許看起來像（寫吧！）像災難）。

說文解詩

　　失去是一種藝術，而且還不難掌握，因為許多事物本身就具有被失去的傾向，像是平日所發生的弄丟鑰匙或虛擲時光等事，地名和人名也是一樣，慢慢都會從人的記憶中消失，所以失去這種藝術本來就不難掌握，因為那是事物的本質和人類的天性。

詞藻釋義

☆ **master** *v.* 熟練，精通
master a technique
精通一種技術

☆ **intent** *n.* 目的，意圖
with intent to do something
意圖做某件事

it is evident that...

詩中用到 it is evident that 句型，這種句型真正的主詞是 that 所引導出來的子句，it 是虛主詞，除了 evident 外，obvious、apparent、clear、noticeable 也可套用到這類句型，都在表達顯而易見之意，不過它們之間還是有些許的不同，使用時要注意。

例句：很顯然的，他們將贏得比賽。

It is apparent that they will win the game.

此時也可用 evident 及上述其他形容詞來代替，把 that 子句擺到句首也行，但虛主詞 it 用不著了——That they will win the game is apparent.

說法有很多方式，有直接的方式，有間接的方式。同樣的，面對自己逐漸喪失的記憶能力，也能以不同的心態對待。

之前講過哀兵策略，女人比較容易心軟，如果自己不是高富帥，也不是富二代或政二代，不妨試試哀兵策略，或許有效。

範例

1
Part

2
Part

3
Part

It is good to be a loser once in a while, but not so good to lose all the time. This is true of a love relationship.

For a man who has been rejected in a love relationship for multiple times, falling in love again could become a psychological barrier for him.

Of course, if the woman is worth all the effort, he will try again despite having doubts that the result might be the same as previous times. You are just the kind of woman that a man will try to win over no matter how hard it might be.

With love.

中譯

　　偶爾失敗是件好事，但老是失敗就不太好了。愛情關係也是如此。

　　對一個在愛情關係上已被拒絕很多次的男人來說，再次愛上一個女人可能會成為一種心理上的障礙。

　　當然如果那個女人值得這一切的努力，他還會再試一次，儘管擔心結果仍會像前幾次一樣。妳就是那種會讓男人不顧艱難全力追求的女人。

　　愛。

知識補給

　　詩人暨短篇小說作家伊莉莎白‧畢夏普（1911-1979）一生獲獎無數，曾在 1949 至 1950 年獲得美國桂冠詩人的頭銜，1956 年得到普立茲文學獎，1970 年再獲得國家圖書獎，可説是集榮耀於一身。儘管如此，畢夏普生前只有出版 101 首詩，1979 年死後名聲更為上漲，有些評論家把她列為美國 20 世紀最重要的作家之一。她是個完美主義者，並不以大量創作為目標，反而不斷花時間在修改作品上，因而作品中呈現出精準的用詞及沈穩的鋪陳。在《一種藝術》中，當遺失或失去成了一種藝術，如果所遺失或失去之物本來就帶有被遺失或失去的意向，那麼失去它們就不會一種災難，因為那些東西本來就會隨著記憶消逝，像是人名、鑰匙、時間、或所待過的城市。

Unit 8
a crowd of / a host of
威廉・沃茲沃斯《我如浮雲般孤獨地漫遊》
William Wordsworth "I Wandered Lonely as a Cloud"

 Classic 經典詩句

I wandered lonely as a cloud
That floats on high o'er vales and hills,
When all at once I saw a crowd
A host, of golden daffodils.

英國浪漫派大詩人威廉・沃茲沃斯（William Wordsworth）在《我如浮雲般孤獨地漫遊》中表達出一種因自然之美而開悟喜樂的心情，著名的詩句為：I wandered lonely as a cloud / That floats on high o'er vales and hills, / When all at once I saw a crowd / A host, of golden daffodils.（我如浮雲般孤獨地漫遊／在山谷之間飄蕩／忽然間我看見一片／金色的水仙花迎風綻放）。

 說文解詩

　　詩人像越過山谷和山丘的孤雲般獨自流浪，突然間在湖邊看到一大片水仙花，這些花隨風擺動，煞是好看。它們就像天上雲河裡綿延不斷的閃爍星星，一眼望去找不到邊際，湖上的水波和水仙花一起擺動跳舞，詩人不知這一切給他帶來怎樣的財富，要到孤寂時心裡再次浮現這些美麗畫面時才知道。

 詞藻釋義

☆ outdo　*v.*　優於，勝過

He tries to outdo his competitor.

他試著勝過對手。

☆ glee　*n.*　歡樂，高興

laugh with glee

哈哈大笑

☆ jocund　*adj.*　歡樂的，快活的

jocund character

快樂的個性

a crowd of / a host of

詩中用 a crowd of 和 a host of 來表示一大片水仙花，英文很多這種表示群體的詞語，用來表示一群人時可用 crowd、group、host、company、gang 等，a crowd of people 就是一群人。

表示獸群可用 herd、colony、drove 等，herd 通常用於許多不同的動物，a herd of 可指 cattle、cows、bulls、oxen、sheep、rams 等動物。

鳥群比較特別，要用 flock 或 flight，如 a flock of birds。另外，一群蜜蜂是 a swarm of bees，一群螞蟻是 a colony of ants。

描寫自然風景時，免不了加入個人感受，但也不能喧賓奪主無病呻吟，還是要以自然為主。

適時引用一些詩句，除了提升自己的氣質外，還可增進彼此間的情趣，但引用的也要是好的詩句才行，或是著名的作品。

範例

I love reading poems.

As a teenager, I was a fan of early 20th-century Chinese poet Xu Zhimo. His work "Taking Leave of Cambridge Again" has been one of my most favorite poems. The first stanza of the poem deeply touches my heart.

It runs as follows: Softly I am leaving, / Just as softly as I came; / I softly wave goodbye / To the clouds in the western sky.

Does it strike you fancy? I want to share it with you because it indicates that we should always cherish our moments together.

With love.

中譯

我喜歡讀詩。

青少年時，我很迷民國初年詩人徐志摩，他所寫的《再別康橋》是我最喜歡的詩作之一，其第一詩節深深打動我的心。

原文如下：輕輕的我走了，／正如我輕輕的来；／我輕輕的招手，／作別西天的雲彩。

有打動妳的心嗎？我與妳分享這首詩，因為它代表我們應該珍惜我們在一起的時刻。

愛。

知識補給

　　由於前面單元已介紹過威廉・沃茲沃斯（1770-1850）的生平，這裡就不再重複。這首《我如浮雲般孤獨地漫遊》一般而言被視為沃茲沃斯最有名的作品，根據英國國家廣播公司（BBC）所做的一項調查，《我如浮雲般孤獨地漫遊》名列全英國從古至今最受喜愛詩作的第五名，可見它受歡迎的程度。民國初年詩人徐志摩曾經留學英國，也受到沃茲沃斯的影響，他的著名詩句「我是天空裡的一片雲」雖不能說是模仿自沃茲沃斯，但總有一點似曾相識之處。徐志摩也翻譯過沃茲沃斯的詩作《露西・葛雷》（Lucy Gray），當時他把這首詩譯為《葛露水》，那是 1922 年，算是徐志摩最早的譯詩。

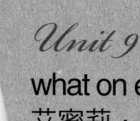

Unit 9

what on earth / why on earth
艾蜜莉·勃朗特《一下下》
Emily Brontë "A Little While"

Classic 經典詩句

The house is old, the trees are bare,
Moonless above bends twilight's dome;
But what on earth is half so dear–
So longed for–as the hearth of home?

19 世紀英國女詩人暨小說家艾蜜莉·勃朗特（Emily Brontë）在這首《一下下》中表達忙裡偷閒時腦裡所浮現的想像世界，著名的詩句為：The house is old, the trees are bare, / Moonless above bends twilight's dome; / But what on earth is half so dear– / So longed for–as the hearth of home?（房子老舊，樹木光禿／往上看是黃昏時刻沒有月光照亮的彎曲蒼穹／地球上有什麼地方比得上家裡的爐火／能有它一半的價值和令人渴望之處？）

　　在繁忙的工作中能稍微休息一下，是一種很大的幸福。詩人一開始就說：一下下，一下下／把累人的工作擺到一旁。接下來可以唱歌可以大笑，但詩人卻問她的心要去哪裡？於是我們進入一個似乎是由記憶所構成的幻想世界。快樂的時光很快過去，又要回到充滿勞動和擔憂的現實世界。

☆ **bare**　　*adj*.　赤裸，光禿

bare feet

光著腳

☆ **dome**　　*n*.　圓頂

the dome of St. Paul's Cathedral in London

倫敦聖保羅大教堂的圓頂

☆ **hearth**　　*n*.　爐邊

He is reluctant to leave hearth and home.

他捨不得離開家和家裡的爐火。

what on earth / why on earth

　　詩中用到 what on earth 這個句型，但不是現在的到底和究竟之意，而是在地球上有什麼。這裡只介紹現在的用法。當有人說"What on earth are you talking about?"，是指「你到底在說什麼？」，而不是「你在地球上說什麼？」。也可用 how on earth 和 why on earth 來表達類似的意思，

　　例句：

　　How on earth did you know that?（你怎麼知道的？）

　　多加 on earth 是為了表示驚訝之意。

　　Why on earth did they bother to do that?（他們幹嘛大費周章去做那事？）

　　作家有敏銳的觀察力，任何事物皆可寫入文章，就是所謂的一沙一世界。

　　情人的世界很小，但不見得視野狹小，因為就算一粒沙中也含有一個世界，問題是你看不看得到，要用心才行。

範例

1
Part

2
Part

3
Part

As English poet William Blake says in one of his poems, "To see a World in a Grain of Sand / And a Heaven in a Wild Flower, / Hold Infinity in the palm of your hand / And Eternity in an hour." We are in a microcosm, where we care for each other. We belong to each other.

I carry your heart with me, and you with mine. We don't need to move out of the small world of lovers into the larger world outside. The reason is that we have already seen a large world in our small one.

With love.

中譯

如英國詩人威廉·布雷克在他的詩中說，「沙中見世界／花中見天堂／掌中握無窮／須臾見永恆」。我們在一個我們兩人相互關懷的小世界裡，相互隸屬。

我隨身帶著妳的心，妳隨身帶著我的心。我們不必從我們的小世界走出到外面更大的世界，原因是我們已經在我們的小世界裡看到一個大世界。

愛。

知識補給

　　説起艾蜜莉‧勃朗特（1818-1848）的詩作，很多人或許不那麼熟悉，但只要提到她的小説《咆哮山莊》（Wuthering Heights），沒聽過的人恐怕很少。更且，她的姊姊夏綠蒂創作出另一世界名著《簡愛》（Jane Eyre），可説是一門雙傑。但她們的家境並不好，由於母親很早過世，必須由擔任副牧師的父親來獨自撫養 6 個小孩。艾米莉和夏綠蒂幾個姐妹曾被父親送到教會學校就讀，但由於受到虐待，類似《簡愛》中的情節。她們幾個小孩就回到家由父親和親戚來教導，像是現在的自學方案，兩位對後世有很大的影響的作家就在這樣的環境下成長茁壯。艾米莉於 1847 年出版她的曠世巨著《咆哮山莊》，不過隔年就因病過世，來不及知道世人對這本小説的反應。

Unit 10
never... without / never... but
艾德格·愛倫·坡《安娜貝·李》
Edgar Allan Poe "Annabel Lee"

Classic 經典詩句

For the moon never beams, without bringing me dreams
Of the beautiful Annabel Lee;
And the stars never rise, but I feel the bright eyes
Of the beautiful Annabel Lee

　　美國文學家艾德格·愛倫·坡（Edgar Allan Poe）在《安娜貝·李》中運用懸疑神秘的氣氛營造出深沈的悲傷，著名的詩句為：For the moon never beams, without bringing me dreams / Of the beautiful Annabel Lee; / And the stars never rise, but I feel the bright eyes / Of the beautiful Annabel Lee（因為月亮一發光，就會讓我夢到／美麗的安娜貝·李／且星星一高掛天空，我就感受到美麗的安娜貝·李／明亮的雙眸）。

 說文解詩

　　這是一首悲傷的詩，發生在很久很久以前一個虛構的海邊王國。敘述者和美麗的女孩安娜貝‧李彼此相愛，愛到連天上的天使都嫉妒，因為天使在天上也過不了這樣快樂的生活。一陣風讓安娜貝‧李受涼生病，終至離開人間。滿懷悲傷的敘述者只能寄情於月光和星光給他帶來的聯想，並終夜睡在安娜貝‧李的墓旁。整首詩到最後才讓讀者知道，原來敘述者是睡在墓旁說這段淒美的故事。

 詞藻釋義

☆ **beam** *v.* 發光，閃光

The sun beams.

太陽光照耀。

重點句型

never... without / never... but

詩中用到 never... without 和 never... but 這兩種類似的句型，雙重否定等於肯定，意思是每怎樣就怎樣。

例句：

He never speaks English without making mistakes.
He never speaks English but he makes mistakes.
兩句都表示他只要一說英文就會說錯。

without 後面要接動名詞，but 作為連接兩個子句的連接詞，所以後面的子句根據前面的子句變化即可。大家熟悉的 It never rains but it pours.就是這種句型。也有人用 It never rains but pours.來表達同樣的意思，此時 but 連接的是兩個動詞。

寫作指引

想像力是寫作的原動力，可虛構出一些不存在的國度或情境，讓讀者神遊其中無法自拔。

一起出去玩可增進彼此的感情，如果又能同時喚起雙方的記憶，豈不更好。在發出邀請時運用一下文字的功力，讓邀約變得更具吸引力。

範例

1 Part

2 Part

3 Part

Have you been to a Disneyland Park anywhere in the world? Like the one in Tokyo.

If you are interested, we could go together. It is a place not just for kids, but also for adults who grew up with Disney movies, such as the "The Lion King" and "Toy Story" in the 1990s.

It is a magical kingdom where you can see all those famous characters and scenes in the same day. I would like to take you there so that we can recapture our childhood memories. It is good to return to childhood once in a while.

With love.

中譯

　　妳有去過全世界任何一個迪士尼樂園嗎？譬如東京迪士尼樂園。

　　如果妳有興趣，我們可以一起去。那裡不是一個只給小孩子玩的地方，對看迪士尼電影長大的成年來說也很具吸引力，這些電影包括 90 年代的《獅子王》和《玩具總動員》。

　　那裡是一個魔法王國，可以讓你在一天之內看到所有在電影裡出現過的角色和場景。我想要帶妳去那裡重溫兒時的回憶，偶而回到童年也是不錯。

　　愛。

知識補給

19 世紀美國作家艾德格・愛倫・坡（1809-1849）在世界文學佔有重要的地位，一方面是因為他是短篇小説這個文類（genre）的開創者之一，另一方面是因為他成功地把心理學元素融入到文學作品之中，營造出懸疑緊張的氣氛，對後世電影的發展有相當的影響，他的短篇小説《告密的心》（The Tell-Tale Heart）最能表現出這種懸疑的氣氛。由於高超的文學技巧，愛倫・坡是美國早期少數能登上世界舞台的作家之一。他在《安娜貝・李》中也運用他擅長的懸疑佈局，像是在海邊塑造出一個如夢似幻的王國，有點像現在電影或動畫中所呈現的畫面。愛倫・坡可以説是走在時代的前端，可惜就像詩中的情節一般，他在愛妻過世後就陷入悲傷，2 年後也隨她而去，享年 40 歲。

Unit 11

at the end
厄尼思特・道森《4月的愛》
Ernest Dowson "April Love"

 **Classic** 經典詩句

We have made no vows--there will none be broke,

Our love was free as the wind on the hill,

There was no word said we need wish unspoke,

We have wrought no ill.

So shall we not part at the end.

19 世紀末英國詩人厄尼思特・道森（Ernest Dowson）在《4月的愛》中論及，若是愛情終要結束，何不快樂地結束。其中著名的詩句為：We have made no vows--there will none be broke, / Our love was free as the wind on the hill, / There was no word said we need wish unspoke, / We have wrought no ill. / So shall we not part at the end.（我們沒有許下任何誓言——也就不會違反誓言／我們的愛像山丘上的風一樣自由／沒有說過我們現在希望沒有說出口的話／我們沒有造成任何傷害／所以我們最後分離。）。

說文解詩

　　這首詩在問，為何不能愉快地結束一場愛情？敘述者說，如果沒有許下任何誓言，分手就不算違背誓言；如果當初沒有說過現在後悔講過的話，那麼分手也就不會造成任何傷害。分手前可以再親一次嘴，然後面帶笑容各奔前程，也就是我們所說的好聚好散。

詞藻釋義

☆ **unspeak** *v.* 取消前言，沒有說

an unspoken promise

沒有明言的承諾

☆ **wrought** *v.* work 的過去式

現在已經很少用，主要出現在聖經的英文譯本中。

現代英語的 work 要以 worked 為過去式。

重點句型

at the end

詩中用到 at the end 這個片語，它和 in the end 很相似，也經常出現在日常對話或文章中，兩者雖然都有最後和最終之意，但用法還是不太一樣。

前者具體表示某東西或地方的尾端或終點，後面通常要加 of 和所指涉的事物或地方，例如：at the end of the street、at the end of the story、at the end of the lesson。

也可表示一段時間的尾聲，如 at the end of the year。

in the end 則只作副詞片語，放在句首或句尾，例如：He caught the bus in the end.

寫作指引

愛情如果太過理性，就會因理性而分手，如果不給承諾，就代表隨時可分手，邏輯上是這樣沒錯。

愛情關係還是要有承諾才能維持下去，沒有承諾的關係只是一種各取所需的隨便關係，說分就分，說散就散，到頭來總是情傷。

範例

1 Part

2 Part

3 Part

A relationship without commitment is a casual relationship. A casual relationship means a lot of things, ranging from hanging out and dining out together to having sex. It is what a lot of young people are doing now.

Does love without commitment exist? This is a question that has been puzzling me. As someone has said, "love is unconditional commitment to an imperfect person." I can't agree more.

Partners in a relationship should learn to tolerate each other's imperfection. I have let you know me as I am. I am naked in front of you.

With love.

中譯

　　沒有承諾的愛情關係是一種隨便的關係。隨便的關係有很多種意義，從一起拍拖和吃飯，到做愛都算。現在很多年輕人都這樣做。

　　沒有承諾的愛可能存在嗎？我一直對這個問題感到困擾。如某人所言：「愛就是對一個不完美的人所做的承諾」。我再同意也不為過。

　　愛情伴侶應該學習相互容忍對方的不完美。我已經讓你了解我真實的一面，我在妳面前是完全的赤裸。

　　愛。

 知識補給

　　厄尼思特‧道森（1867-1900）雖曾就讀牛津大學，但沒有拿到學位。他一生困苦，身體狀況因染有肺病而不佳，加上又有酗酒習慣，且負債累累，32 歲就因重病過世。道森被歸類為世紀末頹廢作家（fin-de-siècle decadent）之一，這類作家的代表性人物為王爾德（Oscar Wilde）。道森的個人行事作風也頗另類，他 23 歲時愛上一個 11 歲小女孩，還向她求婚，結果不成功。根據為道森寫傳記的人的說法，道森有戀童癖傾向，不過他迷戀的不是孩童的身體，而是他們未被社會化污染的清純。他的《4 月的愛》似乎代表了他的愛情觀，4 月象徵年輕及再生的春天，道森渴望年輕時的愛情，可是卻不期待能有快樂的結局。

Learn Smart! 062

學文法，戀習英語寫作：文法佐茶&情詩邂逅

作　　者	許乃文
發 行 人	周瑞德
執行總監	齊心瑀
企劃編輯	魏于婷
校　　對	編輯部
封面構成	高鍾琪

內頁構成	菩薩蠻數位文化有限公司
印　　製	大亞彩色印刷製版股份有限公司
初　　版	2016 年 8 月
定　　價	新台幣 369 元
出　　版	倍斯特出版事業有限公司
電　　話	(02) 2351-2007
傳　　真	(02) 2351-0887
地　　址	100 台北市中正區福州街 1 號 10 樓之 2
E - m a i l	best.books.service@gmail.com
網　　址	www.bestbookstw.com

港澳地區總經銷	泛華發行代理有限公司
地　　　　址	香港新界將軍澳工業邨駿昌街 7 號 2 樓
電　　　　話	(852) 2798-2323
傳　　　　真	(852) 2796-5471

國家圖書館出版品預行編目資料

學文法,戀習英語寫作：文法佐茶&情詩邂逅
/ 許乃文著. -- 初版. -- 臺北市：倍斯特,
2016.08
　面　；　公分. --（Learn smart! ; 62）
ISBN 978-986-92855-4-4(平裝)

1.英語 2.語法 3.寫作法

　　805.16　　　105012993